THE CAVER

The Caver

A NOVEL

CAROL BURNHAM

SOMERVILLE PRESS

Somerville Press Ltd,
Dromore, Bantry,
Co. Cork, Ireland

First published 2014

Designed by Jane Stark
Typeset in Adobe Caslon Pro
seamistgraphics@gmail.com

ISBN: 978 0 9927364 1 5

Printed and bound in Spain
by GraphyCems, Villatuerta, Navarra

for Mark and for Bryan

"…out of rock,
Out of a desolate source,
Love leaps upon its course."

W. B. Yeats

GREEK LESSONS

1

"SO – THIS IS FROM THE WOMAN."

The waiter tossed his head backwards to indicate someone behind him and plunked the heavy white cup of foaming Nescafé on the table.

Claire turned and looked through the stream of pale-skinned tourists pouring down the street between the café and its pavilion where she sat by the low seawall. Then she saw her, the dark, sober proprietress, no longer waiting on tables but sitting at one in the narrow shadow of her café. The woman looked up and smiled. Eleni Pappadopoulos. Claire remembered her from before, her kindness. She also remembered her husband, a severe, hollow-cheeked man who seldom strayed from his stool behind the cash register within. Claire waved her thanks for the coffee, took a swallow and lit up a Greek cigarette, savouring its harsh foreign taste.

The cruise ship anchored at the mouth of Kapsali bay was enormous, out of scale with the rest of the scene. Passengers were still disembarking to the dinghies and then to the pier, from where they marched in droves down the street, delicate cameras beating against their chests like external hearts. Some were renting lounge chairs, intending to go no farther than the pebbly beach. Others entered bars, cafés and souvenir shops. The more adventurous were straying beyond the village and beginning the climb to the Chora. Taxis stood waiting for those who didn't want the trek.

The arrival of cruise ships had begun to spoil the waterfront. There were bars now, several new shops, and the dingy old shops, which before had sold only the necessities for village life, had been refurbished and stacked to their ceilings with useless pottery, chalky statuettes of gods and goddesses, suntan lotions and T-shirts. Claire looked over to Eleni and wondered what she thought about it all.

A cat sprang for a morsel of food on the ground near Claire's feet, one of a gang patrolling the seawall just as they had done years before. John had loved tossing them bits of fish from his plate. More spectator sport than charity, she had thought, studying her husband, for he seemed to relish watching the scramble and frenzied competition for the scraps.

Another group from the boat had entered the pavilion and were seating themselves at the table next to hers. The café was getting crowded. Claire dragged her chair a few feet away, outside the protective awning and into the sunshine—the celebrated light. It was roguish, she thought, kinetic and transforming as it bounced off the water and white stucco walls, bleaching things down to their essence, making, it seemed, an object of the air.

She checked her watch, still on California time, and made the adjustment. It had been over twenty-four hours since she had slept. The boat was leaving at one. To take a walk now might be refreshing, and she could return for lunch when the village was quiet again. Claire worked her feet back into the canvas shoes she had removed and braced them against the seawall to tie the laces. Her naturally pale hands and feet already looked brown against the whitewash. A beginning, she thought, of the immersion she had come for.

She took off in the direction of the pier, turned left and followed the road that ran between a smaller inner bay and a row of white stucco houses. An old stone barracks that once had served as a place of quarantine for sailors still stood at the end of the road. She had completely forgotten about the abandoned building, and seeing it now evoked the strange sensation that the past had simply been put on hold—that it was both tangible and retrievable. There was a path behind it, she remembered now, which John had found one day, leading to the top of the headland overlooking the sea.

Claire stashed her bag in a tuft of grasses, walked the length of the barracks and entered the olive grove behind it. A breeze had come up, rattling the silvery leaves and cooling her skin as she cut a corner through the trees. In the open again, Claire followed John's path upward until, almost halfway to the top of the headland, she spotted a grassy little hillock overlooking Kapsali. There she sat down on a ledge of bedrock and gazed upon the village below, allowing her thoughts of the past to resurface and hold sway.

Their long-ago holiday here seemed to have taken place in another lifetime. Claire's sense of continuity had been unable to survive all the changes that had occurred. Her life had lost its shape and momentum, become fragmented by disruptions and reversals, by two marriages ending in divorce. And now the death of her first husband, Sophie's father. She recalled that little trinity of innocence—mother, father and child. The memory of their final day together kept returning, becoming more, not less, painful with time. The beach picnic, south of San Francisco, to celebrate Sophie's third birthday. John's pathological rage (from where had it come?) when she had refused to share her sandwich with a gull. It had followed a long series of such tantrums provoked by trivial incidents and had been for her the final blow.

In the first months of their marriage she had purchased an album with the idea of creating, over time, a coherent photographic narrative—emblem of a happy life. But the husband-father figure, rather than aging through the pages of years, becoming softer, grayer, dearer, had been cut off while still in his early middle age and eventually replaced by another. Claire had finally removed only the photographs that included Sophie, John and herself and pasted them into a separate album to give to her now grown daughter. The past reshaped, redeemed by narrative. Why not? That was all that remained of it.

When Claire heard the whistle-blast of the boat leaving the harbor, she stood up and watched it take the bend around the cape in the direction of Crete. The port of the Chora was lovely from that height, the scythe-shaped street of small buildings tucked between the rocky hills and glittering water, the long jetty with the small church and turquoise-domed lighthouse on the knoll above it, the ancient fortress

11

rising from the cliff across the bay, looming over it all. And everything that day pale and blurred, seeming to teeter in the numinous light on the edge of nothingness.

The village was now heavy with silence, as if stunned by the sudden evacuation, and the café was empty. She walked up to Eleni, who became animated and extended both hands.

"Claire." She had remembered her name. "How many years? *Poli!*"

"More than twenty."

"You are the same."

"And you."

"How long are you here?"

"I don't know."

"And your husband?"

"He's gone, Eleni." The woman understood her to mean that he had died, which he had, but she had not understood the more complicated thing, that Claire was not his widow. Eleni pursed her lips and shook her head in sympathy.

"Look, Eleni, I have no Greek, but I have books and want to learn. Perhaps you can help me."

"Yes, of course. I will teach."

"But now I need to eat and sleep."

"Where do you stay?"

"Here, *Spitia* Vasili, for now."

"*Orea*. Sit. I will bring you food and wine. Retsina?"

"*Parakalo*."

Claire sat down again by the seawall and watched some children playing in the shallows. A youth had begun gathering and stacking the vacated lounge chairs. The prospect was serene, an aftermath. Suddenly, near the north end of the strand, a man clad in long trousers and shirt came out of the sea, his garments dripping and sagging with the weight of the water. He crossed the beach to where the wall ended and disappeared behind a stand of oleanders. A bird flew up from the shrubbery. Soon she heard the roar of a motorcycle and saw the man take the steep incline out of the village. It was a strange sight, like a dream or an aberration of the trickster light, but she was too weary to question it. She looked back to the children tossing pebbles into the water, and took her first sip of the wine that tastes of pine trees.

2

AFTER LUNCH CLAIRE RETURNED to her bungalow and slipped into crisp, cool bedsheets that smelled of strong soap and sunshine. It was pleasant to fall asleep in the afternoon, shutters closed to the glare, in a room agreeably dim but not dark. She had recently grown afraid of the dark and taken to using a night light. Exhausted by her long journey, she slept through the remainder of the afternoon and evening, waking around midnight to use the bathroom and light another mosquito coil. As she lay down again, she heard voices coming from a few bungalows away, rising with excitement, culminating in loud laughter and then receding into a pool of more subdued and articulated sounds that mingled with the gentle breeze and throbbing song of the cicadas. Just before falling back to sleep, she became aware that they were speaking English.

At first light, she stirred and stared blindly through emerging scraps of consciousness and the scented smoke of the mosquito coil. Then she rose, pushed open the shutters and leaned against the sill to take in the sights and sounds of Kapsali. Perhaps it was the long sleep or the strangeness of waking up in a foreign place, but that morning seemed to her particularly keen, its light more than natural sunlight. She could barely remember the day before. A white-winged swallow arrowed through the cool fresh air to a muddy nest under the eaves of a nearby bungalow, and gulls screeched over the bay. The fishing boats were coming in after their morning runs, and she would have let the rhythm of their overturning motors lull her back into sleep had she not arranged for a taxi. Yiannis would be arriving in less than an hour to take her to the Chora for supplies.

She entered the kitchen alcove, filled the *briki* with water, turned the valve on the canister of gas and lit a match. There were only two burners and a minuscule oven, a marked contrast to her California kitchen with its yards of granite counter, special wine refrigerator and commercial stove. She took her coffee to the front porch and sat down. The porches of the bungalows at *Spitia* Vasili afforded a view of the bay, more interesting for being broken by the delicate tracery of pine boughs and the testicular clusters of cones. The forecourt was almost completely in the shadow of the pines, while the area behind the bungalows remained open to the sun and studded with old olive trees, whose gnarled, low-spreading branches pinned their shadows close around them.

"Excuse me, is anybody home?"

Claire had returned from the Chora early and was just putting on her swimsuit with the intention of going to the beach when the female voice came through the window that opened on the porch. She cringed at the American accent, imagining her visitor to be a cruise ship passenger, though she hadn't heard the whistle-blast. Then came an insistent knocking at the door. Grumbling, Claire put on a long T-shirt and opened the door a crack.

"I'm very sorry to disturb you. Are you the American?" Standing before her was a beautiful young woman in very high heels and a sober gray suit, obviously not a tourist. Claire opened the door all the way and motioned for her to enter. "Oh, no, thank you," said the woman, running her fingers through the dark roots of her dyed hair, a thatch of bright orange-red. She seemed overheated and exasperated. "I just wondered if you know where Stella, uh, *Kyria* Vasili is. I came back from work to get some forms I'd forgotten and then realized I'd locked myself out—oh, I'm sorry. I'm Zoe Stefanides. I live just down there." She sighed and pointed to her bungalow, in the area from which the voices had drifted the night before.

"I'm Claire. Claire—Paxton." She always faltered when it came to her last name, having been through three of them and recently returning to her maiden one. "The *Kyria* is in Potamos today. She mentioned it yesterday." Claire looked at her watch. Eleven. "She won't be back until later this afternoon. But perhaps—are there any open windows?"

"Only the high one."

"Hmm, I noticed a ladder yesterday when I was moving in. Follow me." They walked around to the rear of her bungalow where, as Claire had remembered, a ladder lay horizontally against the twisted trunk of one of the olives. Each taking an end, they picked it up and marched along the pine-needled path. While Claire held it firmly against the window, Zoe kicked off her shoes, stepped quickly up the ladder and hoisted herself head-first through the small opening. Her stockinged feet swayed comically for a few seconds on the window frame before disappearing. Leaving the ladder, Claire walked around to the front and up the steps, high heels in hand.

"I can't thank you enough." Zoe took the shoes, slipped her feet into them, and straightened her skirt.

"Your English led me to believe you were a tourist. I almost didn't open the door. Uncharitable of me I know."

"No. I understand. They're like wasps let out of a box. As for my English, I lived in the States. I went to medical school in San Francisco."

"That's where I'm from."

"I know. Stella mentioned you were coming."

"You're a doctor."

"Yes. I've been assigned to this island for my year's government service. My office or what is called the 'clinic' is up in the Chora." Zoe glanced over to Claire's cellphone lying on the counter. "And, by the way, I have a telephone, if you ever want to use it. The island isn't equipped yet for wireless."

"Well, a doctor, one who speaks English, and a telephone nearby. What luck. " Claire turned to go, and Zoe followed her down the stairs, the forgotten forms in hand. "By the way, did I hear English coming from this porch last night?"

"Yes. We were speaking English for our Maltese friend. His English, you see, is better than his Greek. The other people, Zeno and Alexandra Ladas, are Greek—artists, but they've spent some time in England. You should meet them. We're having dinner there tomorrow and Alex is always encouraging me to invite others. Would you like to come?" Zoe and Claire walked back up the path.

"Oh, thank you, no. I don't quite know how to say this, but I think I need to be alone for a while."

"Yes, that's often true of people coming here. They don't want more of—what they're running away from. Oh, sorry, perhaps I—."

"No, don't apologize. I am escaping, and I do want some solitude. But I'm not a recluse, and I'm very glad to have met you."

"Well, feel free to change your mind." Zoe waved goodbye with the papers and pointed towards her car, parked up on the road. "I mean about tomorrow night."

Back in her bungalow, Claire tossed cigarettes, lotion, towel and a bottle of water into a plastic bag and set out for the beach. Halfway up the main road that linked the port to the Chora, she turned left on a gravelled track that followed along a deep gorge and ended at the site of an abandoned construction project—the shell of a half-completed hotel, an unplumbed pool and two stone cottages—where before there had been just rock and scrub. She had seen the larger structure from Kapsali. Unfinished projects were plentiful here. The architecture of Greece was a deconstructed one, she thought, of columns without walls and walls without roofs, features of both the incomplete-new and the ruined-ancient, the broken and linear suggesting, curiously, their opposites—the complete and cyclical.

She followed the path leading gently downhill from the building site to the edge of the promontory and then, very cautiously, descended the steep path cut into the slope behind the cove that ended in large boulders. These she climbed down to flatter surfaces of rock, on which she could walk upright to the stony beach. A stiff breeze was stirring the water, bringing it to symmetrical pointy waves like a child's drawing of the sea. She took off her T-shirt, placed it with her bag on a handy shelf of rock, and made her way over the larger pebbles to the shingle. There she removed her shoes and sat down, burying her feet in the tiny stones beneath the water.

The tide pulling at the shingle of the sloping shore created a gentle, grating sound. Dreamily she gathered handfuls of the wet stones and let them slip through her fingers, enjoying their cool smoothness. There were some pleasing yellow and red ones among the plainer grays. She put a few of the larger ones aside, thinking she might decorate her bungalow. Then she remembered the lesson of Thoreau—the rock he would have to dust—so she threw them one by one into the water, relishing the symbolism of the act as well as the clear plopping sound they made. It was a lovely little inlet, intimate, with protective tall walls of rock on either side extending far beyond the shoreline. Claire knew that, as summer progressed, tourists renting pedalboats on Kapsali beach would poke into this small cove just as cruise ships did the harbor. For a while, though, it would be hers.

A wind had suddenly come up and the inlet was now a cauldron of roiling water, splashing hard and high against the rock. Deciding not to swim, Claire moved farther back on the beach and, using her T-shirt as a pillow, lay down on the sun-warmed pebbles. She closed her eyes and fell into a half-sleep. The sounds of the wind and water, distorted by the cove's peculiar formation of land and sea, created strange, sibilant echoes, sounding at times like the human voice.

She could hear Sophie's voice. Sophie, the baby who had been here with her, a woman now and a mother herself. Claire had observed that the lighthouse above the pier, with its modified hour-glass shape, resembled the new type of baby bottle that Sophie had used for Annabel, even to its dome above the loggia that looked like a bright blue nipple. Sophie's voice, soft, disapproving, condescending at times. Her life would be seamless, not broken up as her mother's had been. She had used the past tense, as if Claire's life were over. Claire had laughed joylessly at that. She was only forty-six. Her own life, her daughter insisted, would be integrated and harmonious, like one of her room designs, like a work of art. The only thing her mother had "together," she cruelly said once, were her stories. Sophie had suffered.

The day after the picnic Claire had resolutely packed her suitcase, rolling up Sophie's tiny items of apparel and tucking them around the edges, written the hasty note, and left. The legal term was "desertion." And now John's recent death had fostered in her a new and frightening perspective, one from which she saw her long-ago act as unpardonably callow and cruel (perhaps his rages had been a harbinger of the disease to come), her feelings for him as deep and lasting (or was the posthumous rebirth of a long ago love a false thing?), and the impossiblity of ever knowing either and, worse, feeling fundamentally to blame. She felt she had forsaken him.

"Don't do it." Sophie's voice again, advising her mother against this last divorce. "Your life is good now, stable. You have everything you want." Sophie had decorated the house Claire had left behind. She had always done that, even as a little girl, dragging weeds and flowers inside during the spring and summer, leaves and pods in the autumn. A progression of Sophies ran through Claire's mind: the baby, the little girl, the conservative teenager admonishing her mother. The stages of life are telescoped by the metamorphoses of ancient myth, she reflected, but also by a mother's memory. *Which of her forms has shown her substance right?* Claire said the words aloud, remembering the line from her favorite poet.

She opened her eyes and sat up. The wind had stopped, and the water was still and shiny, opalescent, as if its active surface had been smoothed out by plastic wrap. She took off her swimsuit, stepped over the pebbles to the water's edge and into the shallows. When the water reached her thighs, she fell in and did a fast crawl around a boulder whose top came close to the surface, and then out to where the rock walls ended and released the cove waters to the open sea. Here she turned over and floated, giving herself up to the gentle current, letting it take her where it would. Claire could barely make out the baby-bottle lighthouse across the bay, and the little church beside it looked like an enormous hunk of goat cheese. Her gaze travelled back to the cove with the abandoned hotel above it. The west walls of the two unfinished cottages, rough mosaics of cream, rose and orange stone, followed the cliff line. There was movement in the window of one of them, a slice of white against the blackness. Swallows, she supposed, nesting within.

Back on the beach she quickly dressed. She was hungry, and her skin prickled from salt and sunburn. As she climbed the boulders upwards in the direction of the path, she noticed, just above her handhold, a bright little flower growing out of a crevice in the rock. Its stiff stem was silvery and leafless and its face a tight cluster of tiny yellow straw-like buds. It was the type sold in bunches in kiosks and tourist shops all over Greece, but she had never seen it in its natural state. She would ask someone for the name. Names were important to her.

When she reached the top of the embankment, she saw she hadn't been alone. A young man was scrambling away from the hotel, and there was something about his posture and the way he scuttled across the uneven ground that struck her as peculiar. He was bent forward, as if ready to use his arms. That was it. He moved with the ease of an animal familiar with its terrain. Claire wondered what he could be doing there.

It was late afternoon. Claire had eaten lunch at Eleni's café, then showered and napped. The village was still asleep and would not stir until evening. The only sounds were the distant drone of a fishing boat and the metallic warbling of swallows just outside her window. Her thoughts turned to the little yellow flower, its namelessness. A name, a single word, could somehow penetrate the mystery of a thing. She believed in words. Language was the mediator between us and the objective world.

Eleni had been at her café as usual, sitting against the wall in the sunshine. The Greek woman intrigued her. There was an unwavering stillness about her, a solidity that made Claire feel flimsy, almost immaterial. And Eleni seemed to possess a strange consonance with the island, seeming as much a part of it as the rocks and trees. Claire had known she would write here, and now she believed she had found her subject.

3

THERE WAS A TENTATIVE RAP on the bungalow door. Eleni was five minutes early. Claire put down her book of Greek verbs.

"*Kalispera.*"

"*Kalispera. Ti kanete?*" Good evening. How are you? Claire now knew the basic greetings. The Greek woman, smiling diffidently, brushed the dark hair away from her face and took Claire's offered hand.

"*Kala, eseis?*" Fine, and you?

"*Kala.*"

"Shall we sit outside? It's still light."

"*Ne.*" The counterintuitive nay, meaning "yes" here.

"Ouzo, coffee?"

"*Ne. Kafés, parakalo.*"

Claire poured Eleni a tiny cup of the muddy Turkish-type coffee that the Greeks prefer and herself a glass of ouzo. She then handed both drinks to the woman to carry and, balancing books, paper, pen, mosquito repellent and a package of cigarettes, ushered her out to the porch. The air was lovely, warm and embracing, infused with the scent of pine. She lit the citronella candle and a cigarette, inviting Eleni with a sweeping gesture to sit down. She couldn't remember the Greek word, *kafit*—something.

"Cigarette?"

"No thank you. I don't smoke."

"Or drink alcohol?"

"Oh, yes, sometimes. But I don't like ouzo. Thank you, Claire. I don't like anise."

"It's beautiful out tonight."

"*Orea.*"

"Yes, *orea.*" What a beautiful word for "beautiful," the '*r*' pronounced with the softening involvement of the tongue, as it is in Spanish. The lessons were going well. They would begin with the amenities in Greek—for most of these Claire had mastered—followed by a recitation or a writing task agreed upon the meeting before, the alphabet, a categorical list, or the conjugation of some verbs. Afterwards, they would simply converse in English, with the plan of lapsing into Greek as Claire became able. That night she recited the numbers to one hundred and, in review, wrote the Greek alphabet in small letters. When they had finished the formal part of the lesson, Claire put her feet on the low porch wall and lit another cigarette.

"Why are you here?" Eleni asked in Greek.

"Because I long for something I have known and want back again," Claire whispered without hesitation, more to herself than to Eleni. She didn't know what the "something" was. Eleni looked confused and repeated the question in English.

"That's all right. I understood the Greek."

"*Then perazi*. Never mind."

"No, I want to answer your question—the word for 'question'?"

"*Eroteethe*."

"Thank you—*efaristo*. I want to answer your question. For myself as well." She noticed Eleni's empty cup and stood up. "More coffee?"

"*Tipota*. Nothing, *efaristo*." Claire took her own glass to the kitchen and returned with more ouzo. "My life is a shambles, Eleni."

"Shambles?"

"Uh, sorry, chaos." She could always rely on the words of Greek origin. "I've had two husbands, three lives."

Eleni made a little sound, unable to disguise her surprise.

"I should be at the beginning of a contented middle age, but I'm not content. Why am I here? For rest, I think, and answers."

"*Kai ee koreesou*—and your daughter?"

"She is happy. All grown-up, beautiful, married with a daughter of her own. My granddaughter, Annabel."

"Ah, bravo."

"And you, Eleni, how many children?"

"*Oxi—tipota.*" The woman put forefinger to thumb to make a zero, then blushed and looked down at the empty cup cradled in her lap. By then it was dark, and all that could be seen beyond the porch where they sat were the other dimly lit porches and the huge silhouettes of the pines against a brilliant star-strewn sky. Voices were coming from Zoe's porch, another gathering of her friends.

"Oh, Eleni, I've been meaning to ask you something. When I go swimming at the little beach below the unfinished hotel, there's always a man there, a young man. Is he a caretaker or guard? He never seems to be working."

"You see the voyeur." Eleni smiled.

"The what?"

"'Voyeur.' A French word."

"*Ne,* I know, we use it too. There isn't a good English equivalent. But how strange."

"He does that since he was twelve. Now he's twenty-one or -two. He does no harm. We laugh about it. It's the tourists, I think. All the women on the beach in bikinis. Everybody knows about it, but not his family."

"Who are his family?"

"You know the house. On the road to Chora. The house with goats and a little black dog."

"Oh, yes, I've seen the mother." Claire remembered the short plump woman with a moustache, hanging out clothes to dry. "How sad." She recalled then the movements in the cottage window that she had been thinking were nesting swallows. Of course. The young man had been spying on her.

"I go now," Eleni said, rising. Her departures were always abrupt.

"What's his name—the young man's?"

"Dimitri. Thank you for the coffee. Good night."

"*Avrio. Efaristo poli.*"

Claire sat down again and lit another cigarette. The tightness in her throat reminded her that she had to quit smoking—but not yet. The voices were still coming from Zoe's porch. Their conviviality was like a tisane, diffusing contentment and cheer through the warm dark air. They were more subdued that night, and the words were unintelligible— soothing, as Claire remembered her parents' conversation having been before she was old enough to understand the words. When the mystery was still intact. Is it that we all want back again? She sat for an hour or more, taking in the Mediterranean night—the smell of cigarette smoke and pine, the music of cicadas and happy people. When the human sounds had subsided, she went back inside and picked up her pen.

Many of Eleni's relatives had taken part in Kythera's resistance during World War II, including three of her mother's uncles, who had been murdered by German soldiers. Her grandfather had also fought but managed to escape the execution line-up and hide in a cave below Kalamos. It had been a dark time, occurring more than a decade before her birth, and one to which her mother seldom referred, so she did not want to be reminded of it in history class. But she loved the ancient tales of her island. They lit up the past and gave her a sense of having a personal history that preceded by many years her actual birth. The stories made her feel as if she had been on earth almost as long as a goddess.

For centuries Kythera had been fought over like a precious jewel and won by a series of foreign invaders—the Romans, the Venetians, the French, the Turks, the British, a list as long as Homer's catalogue of ships. But when Eleni gazed down at the sea from the headland above Kapsali, her thoughts travelled to a time long before those invasions. The Phoenicians had sailed their great ships around the cape and into Kapsali bay to harvest a tiny sea snail for its purple dye, and she imagined enormous purple sails flapping in the wind against a pearly pink sky and turquoise sea. The island was purple, she thought, was even called "Porphyris," before the murex disappeared and it turned red with blood.

Although she loved ancient history and English, Eleni hated and was well on her way to failing mathematics. It was for that reason her mother believed her when, wanting to leave for the Chora early on Tuesdays, Eleni had said she was being tutored in the subject before classes began. At the first sound outside her window, her grandfather clearing his throat and shuffling across the small inner yard to the outdoor toilet, she was out of bed and shaking her mother, who slept in the bed next to hers. She quickly climbed into her blue and white uniform and entered the kitchen, where she tore off a piece of yesterday's bread and spread it with the soft white cheese from the milk of their goats. Then she took the brush, comb, and a small bowl of water to her mother, who was only half-awake and sitting on the rug that covered her bed.

Eleni drew up a chair and sat down imperiously with her back to her mother, holding a hand mirror in front of her. She wore her long dark hair in one of three ways, a single braid down the back, two braids, or, her favorite, an elaboration of the second, in which the braids were brought up and wound around her head. She wore it that way on Saturday nights when they went to the taverna, and although today was only Tuesday, she pleaded with her mother for that style.

Eleni looked at her image critically. She was twelve and just beginning to think about her appearance. For the last year, she had been observing the faces and shapes of her female classmates and drawing comparisons with her own. She thought she was ugly, or at least not as beautiful as her classmate Pelagia. She gazed at the thin dark oval with the well-defined brows and small bright eyes. Her mother had said it was a "nice" face, but she had never heard that said about Pelagia's. Her teeth were a problem, oversized and slightly protruding, and she was in the habit of covering her mouth with her hands when she smiled. One day she had taken the mirror out to the garden and, sitting on a small chair among the chickens and geraniums, had practised smiling with her lips closed. At least her angular body, which made her feel awkward when she was with her shorter, rounder friends, was taking on a new, more womanly shape.

She gathered her books and, throwing kisses to her mother and grandfather, set out for Kapsali. She walked rapidly downhill on the donkey path, which wound around white bee boxes and stalks of wild artichoke, skipping from time to time to increase her speed. The sun at her back bathed the village below, its freshly white-washed houses and shops, in a soft orange light. She stopped for a moment to readjust her book bag, fashioned by her mother from a small Turkish rug, and unbuttoned the top button of her blouse, lifting the collar so it would stand up around her neck. Her Australian cousin, Serena, had done that on her visit the summer before.

The Italian fishing boat always came in between seven and seven-thirty. That morning, as every Tuesday morning, the five men leapt one at a time from the rusty old vessel to the jetty and, happy to be on land again, took long, energetic strides towards the taverna, where they could buy bread, beer, coffee, cigarettes and gasoline. As they approached the building, they came upon the Greek girl standing in the partial shade of a paint-splattered oleander. She was shyly looking up at them and smiling her well-rehearsed, tooth-concealing smile. "Koritsimou, kalispera!" they shouted in unison, laughing and feigning surprise. The men carried with them samples of their catch, one holding a bucket of tiny silver fish, which sparkled in the sunlight, and a large, stiff, newspaper-wrapped fish under his arm like a loaf of bread. Four of them were old, three as old as her mother and one even as old as her grandfather, but the fifth—she had heard them call him Carlo—was only eight or ten years older than she was.

Carlo looked like a god from her mythology book. He had curly hair, honey-colored skin, and teeth as white as a row of eggs. As always, he looked straight into her eyes and handed her an anise-flavored candy. There was something about his look that made her feel funny down low in her belly. No one had ever looked at her that way. Every day she dreamed of marrying Carlo and sailing away to the magical land that would be as beautiful as the sea path leading to it. Italia. She liked the way the word rolled off her tongue.

THE ICON

4

Several days after their meeting, Zoe invited Claire to her bungalow. The doctor was late coming home from work, and they met at the bottom of her steps. Zoe led the way up to the porch, gestured for Claire to sit down and went inside. She appeared a few minutes later with a decanter of retsina and a small dish of black olives, which she placed with a flourish on the metal table. The sun had left their end of Kapsali in shadow, and they watched as it lit up the church and lighthouse and moved across the bay to disappear, in a brilliant splash of red, behind the old fortress.

"I don't care what they say, this stuff is good." Claire poured herself a second glass of the retsina.

"And you can drink gallons of it with no hangover. They must water it. Would you excuse me for a minute? I want to get out of these clothes." Zoe was wearing the same suit and high heels she had worn the day they had broken into her bungalow. She reappeared barefoot in a chenille robe, sighed as she sat down again and put her feet on an adjacent chair. The robe fell away to expose a pair of thin, shapely legs. "That's better. Where were we?"

"Nowhere, happily. Just watching the sun go down." Claire had felt from the beginning an understanding with Zoe. They were already like old friends resting easily in their silences. "Do you mind if I smoke?" Claire asked. She had not yet seen Zoe light up.

"Of course not. I was thinking—. I have an appointment tomorrow in Myrtidia to meet the priest. Why don't you come with me? If you haven't been to the monastery there, you should go. It's lovely."

"The priest?"

"Part of my job," Zoe said, chuckling at Claire's surprise. "As the government doctor, I'm supposed to introduce myself to the island clergy.

There will be times when we'll have to work together, you know—the final
scenes. The ambassadors of the body and soul must meet in preparation
for the comforts of the sick and dying." A human coherence that was very
Greek, Claire thought, and she agreed to accompany Zoe on her mission.

The next morning Yiannis brought his taxi to a halt in front of an
almond orchard. Zoe had arranged for them to be dropped off halfway
so they could continue their excursion on foot and be picked up later
at the monastery. The women set out on a flat and newly paved road,
walking at a brisk clip through the countryside, and Claire soon became
lost in the rhythmic beat of their shoes against the pavement and the
rumble of the still invisible sea below. They passed a schoolhouse in a
large shady yard, a farmhouse with a sign announcing honey for sale,
and now were coming upon a graveyard. Glass jars of plastic flowers in
unnatural colors sat on or beside concrete coffins, nestled in overgrown
grasses. There might be some solace, Claire thought, in the prospect of
being placed after death above the ground, still in the sun. *On* the earth,
not *in* it—what a difference a preposition could make.

A dark cloud of insects had appeared out of nowhere, as if Pandora's
box had been lurking among the coffins. "Horseflies," Zoe hissed,
swatting at one. Several were flying around Claire, trying to land, and
when they did, they seemed to stick. She jumped all over the road,
flapping her arms dementedly. Zoe laughed. "You see, the wind has
stopped. That's why they're out. There's a village around the next bend
where we can rest for a while." They broke into a run, finally freeing
themselves of the pursuing swarm. When they reached the village,
they begged two iced coffees from a proprietor who was closing his
café. No one else was in sight, the inhabitants having already taken
refuge from the noonday heat. They sat down opposite the café on
a low stone wall, which was shaded by a plane tree and the rounded
apse of a church. Enjoying the rest and the cooler air, neither said a
word until they had finished their drinks.

"You know, Claire, I haven't been here much longer than you have. Just a few weeks. But I've already learned a lot about some of the islanders."

Claire was about to ask Zoe if she had met Eleni Pappadopoulos when she stopped herself, thinking it would be more interesting, at least for a while, to simply imagine her subject's life. Later she could infuse her imaginings with facts as she gathered them and watch how life and narrative intersected. She would investigate that mystery.

"Gossip is rampant in a place like this," Zoe continued. "In some ways, you're lucky to be an outsider, an observer, objectifying, not really understanding. Like a camera."

"I know what you mean. The language, for instance, has a beautiful almost lapidary quality that is lost once we begin to understand some of the words. Any language we don't know exists for us purely as rhythm and sound. I find it strangely comforting listening to conversations I don't understand. I think that's because they take me back to the half-conscious contentment of infancy." Claire thought of John's diagnosis. *The words go first*. Could the unravelling of Alzheimer's return one to that place? Was there contentment in that wordless place or was it, as Iris Murdoch had feared, a highly conscious and, therefore, brutal "sailing into darkness"?

Zoe looked at her watch. "Claire, sorry, but I think we'd better get going or we'll be late." They returned the tumblers to a small table against the taverna wall, as they had been instructed to do, and set out again, moving from the cool shade of the village into the glare. Now the road began its descent, and the breeze had picked up again, a brisk crosswind chopping up the sea that lay before them. There were no more horseflies, and the loud chirring of the remaining insects seemed a celebration of their endurance and collusion with the wind.

"Speaking of 'observers,'" Claire said, recalling Zoe's earlier remark. "Did you know the island has a voyeur?"

"My guess is that there're more than one. Islands breed strange people. But, no, I didn't know. There is a murderess. I wouldn't mention it were it not for your outsider status and the fact that she'll be serving us lunch today." Zoe seemed to savour the shock value of her declaration. "She's from Crete, where she murdered her young children forty or more years ago. Now she looks after the priest."

Half an hour later they walked through the tall wooden doors of the monastery into a sunny courtyard, enclosed by the high, bougainvillea-covered church wall and an L-shaped low building with a series of uniform brown doors. A tall pine shaded part of the yard, and the pavers were strewn with the tree's fallen brown needles and cones, as well as stacks of upended terracotta pots. A loud animal screech pierced the silence. Claire was about to ask Zoe what it was when a woman appeared in the courtyard to welcome them. Zoe and the guide exchanged some words, and the latter ducked into one of the brown doors, returning with two coarsely woven skirts for the guests. Taking her cue from Zoe, Claire stepped into hers, drawing its loose elastic waist up over her shorts. The woman then took them around the corner of the church and through a breezy portico, which overlooked grounds sloping to the sea, a long, gentle descent through scattered shrubs and brush. There Claire saw the source of the cry she had heard. A fat peacock was flapping clumsily through the air, his feathers twinkling in the sunlight. It landed nearby in a bushy white oleander.

The guide unlocked the door to the church with an iron key and stood aside for them to enter. They passed through the cool, dark vestibule, their footsteps echoing profanely against the tile floor. It was like entering a cave, Claire thought. It occurred to her then that the early churches might have been fashioned after caves, the hanging votive lamps in copper or brass filigree imitating a cavern's limestone formations. The chapel smelled of metal polish, candlewax and stale incense. "I was told it's customary for visitors to come here first," Zoe explained. "Afterwards we meet the priest." She took Claire's wrist, and they approached the iconostasis. Claire had seen a number of icons, but the "Myrtidiotissa" was unusual, larger than most, about four feet tall, almost as wide, and gold-chased. The gold gleamed in the single shaft of sunlight coming through the open door.

"It looks valuable," Claire remarked, thinking "gaudy." Yet lyrical too, she thought, not unlike the Greek churches themselves.

"It is valuable," Zoe said, "its age and, of course, the gold. During the German occupation, it was hidden in the church basement." The draped, crowned figures of the madonna and child, in the medieval style less an infant than a diminutive man, the winged angels treading air in the upper corners, the three more prosaic images at the bottom—a fortress, a church, a shepherd tending his flock—were all hammered and etched in gold, drawing the eye to the part that was not. The face of the madonna was a black, featureless oval.

"There's a story," Zoe whispered. "Turkish pirates came ashore, maybe Barbarossa himself, and burned the face of the original." Eastern negation one way or the other, Claire mused, if not theological then piratical. Or—.

"It might have been the artist himself," she ventured. She found the blank countenance of the virgin the most interesting thing about it. "Perhaps he was reluctant to put a human face on something abstract, on—the divine."

Zoe sighed, obviously preferring the pirate version. As Claire stood there looking at the icon, she was warming to her own idea. She thought of the biblical proscription of graven images, Islam's injunctions, even Plato's. Then she remembered that iconography was a conservative art, a copying rather than an inventive one.

Zoe genuflected, made the sign of the cross, and dropped some coins in the offertory.

Father Viacouras greeted them at the entrance to the refectory and led them to the far side of the room near the kitchen. He was a large, red-faced man in his forties, a sensual man, Claire surmised, as she watched him fondle and smooth his long graying beard against his chest. He looked shrewd as well. The heavy dark brows sloping to his cheekbones gave his bright black eyes a parenthetical aspect, as if the cunningness there should be overlooked in favor of the priestly trappings—the cassock, *skoufos* and beard.

A moon-faced old woman with some missing teeth appeared and fussed about the long oak table, one of many in the plain room. Claire stared at the plump hands that had killed her own children. The woman retreated into the kitchen and returned with the first bowl of steaming lamb's head soup, bowing and placing it before the priest, after which she served the guests. When Father Viacouras turned away to give the servant some further instructions, Claire pointed with alarm to the two-toned gelatinous sphere floating in her broth. Zoe suppressed a giggle. "The eye," she whispered. "It's an honor. Eat it." The priest reached greedily for the bread, guzzled some wine, and looked lustfully at Zoe. Claire, observing that his English was poor, urged them to speak in their own language.

After lunch, the women thanked the priest and made their way back through the courtyard to the entrance. At the gate, they shed their skirts and returned them to the guide. The taxi was waiting, and they climbed in. "I didn't think I was going to get that damned eye down my throat!" Claire exclaimed as they pulled away.

"*Mayeritsa* is an Easter tradition here, but maybe they have it more often in monasteries. It's probably very economical."

"Tell me more about the 'Myrtidiotissa,'" Claire said. "Is the region and monastery named for her, or the reverse?"

"She's the madonna found in the *myrtia*. The story goes that the icon we just saw, or its original, was discovered by a shepherd in a myrtle bush. He removed it several times, only to find it every time mysteriously back in the same place. So it was there, at the site of the bush, that the islanders built her a church. Of course she has worked many miracles. The first was curing a man of paralysis. There's a huge celebration every August twenty-fourth in her honor. Most of the celebrants and pilgrims who come here on retreat seek cures, especially for infertility."

Claire rolled down the window to let in some air and wondered what the spirit of "Myrtidiotissa" might do for emotional paralysis, for guilt, for fear of the dark.

5

It was mid-July before Claire finally accepted one of the many invitations to accompany Zoe to dinner at the Ladases' house, near the inland village of Livadi. Zoe's "please come" as she took Claire's hands in hers on the day before the event seemed to have a special urgency. That evening, Zoe drove to the turquoise-domed Byzantine church in Kato Livadi, turned left and followed a dirt-and-gravel road for what seemed to be miles. Finally, they entered a private driveway that led through an opening in a copse of trees hiding the house from the road.

Alex Ladas, fiftyish, gentle-faced, and comfortably overweight, came bounding out the front door to welcome them. Claire recognized her at once as a woman she had often seen with her husband at Eleni's café. She wore a full, gathered skirt and elaborately embroidered blouse. Her long dark-gray hair was secured at the nape of her neck with a wide tortoise-shell barrette. Zeno stood in the doorway. His shock of unruly white hair, baggy clothes, and benign, abstracted expression reminded Claire of photographs she had seen of Albert Einstein. Alex took Claire's hand and pulled her into the house, through the sitting room, which also served as a dining room, and into the fragrant kitchen. She presented her with an artichoke canapé and a jelly-glass of red wine. "Come," she said then, putting an arm around Claire's waist and guiding her out the back door, across a small patio to the studio.

The studio had been a century-old stable, Alex explained, the only building on the land they had bought several years before. They had converted it and lived and worked in it while their house was being built. The thick earth-colored walls and roughly hewn wooden beams of the new house blended well with this original structure. Alex opened the small, heavy door and preceded Claire into the room. It was not yet dark, and the unframed paintings, hanging chock-a-block along the walls, seemed to glow in the bluish light falling from a canted skylight above. Claire found it difficult to focus on any single work, for it was jointly that they seemed to make their impact, Alex's representative forms and Zeno's abstract compositions mingling in a profound statement of creation. Alex looked to her guest for a response.

"They're beautiful," Claire said, at once regretting the blandness of the remark. She strolled around the perimeter of the room, stopping from time to time, pleased by an image. "Where do you find room for new ones?" There was no spare wall space.

"Oh, we always make room, selling them as quickly as we create them. We own a small gallery in Crete and also have two buyers, one in London and one in Athens. The Athenian buyer will be with us this evening."

"But they're perfect now, this particular mix. How can you bear to change anything?" Claire walked over to an easel at one end of the room, on which rested an unfinished canvas, obviously Alex's, surrounded by smelly rags. She sneezed, a reaction she always had to the smell of turpentine.

"It just works. I don't know why. But the combination is constantly changing— one of the gratifying things. That, by the way, is Daphne."

"What did you say?" Claire turned to Alex, who was standing behind her, pointing to the canvas.

"The painting. It's going to be Daphne, the wood nymph. But I'm having some problems with it." The artist found a stray strand of hair and tucked it behind her ear. Claire had noticed she did this habitually, even when there wasn't hair in her face.

"Oh yes, I see now." Claire moved closer to the easel. It was Daphne in the process of becoming a tree. One arm, raised in flight, was leafing out. Claire was fascinated by the unfinished work, the rich color of its completed details, the arm, part of the torso and face, floating outwards from the muted background, from the nothingness of the barely visible pencil strokes on white. "It's getting a little dark in here. Is there a light perhaps?"

"No, we work only in natural light. Let's join the others now."

Alex and Claire returned to the house where the aromas wafting from the kitchen had intensified and become identifiable as roasting lamb and potatoes. Zeno refilled their glasses, and Alex lit some candles around the room, including those in a wrought-iron chandelier hanging over the oval dining table. It was covered in a red handwoven fabric and set haphazardly, the utensils at odd angles and various lengths from the table's edge, some of the napkins folded, others not.

"We do have electric light in here, of course," Alex explained, looking like a clumsy bee as she moved quickly from candle to candle, "but this is nicer."

"And then no one notices if the meat is too rare," Zeno said, smiling. There was a loud rap at the door, and he opened it, backing away slightly as if shrinking from an expected gust of wind. Byron Velisarios, the Athenian art dealer, entered briskly with his wife, Mina, whose strong floral perfume immediately filled the room. She handed Alex a square cardboard box wrapped in string and kissed Zoe on both cheeks. They made a striking couple, the art dealer robust and self-assured, his wife vivacious and beautiful, despite excess weight. Behind them was someone else, whom Zeno ushered into the room and introduced. Claire thought the new arrival, a slight, seemingly diffident man, might be the Maltese to whom Zoe had referred weeks before, the man for whom she and the Ladases had spoken English as they sat on her front porch in the moonlight.

They arranged themselves around the table, and Alex brought in a large platter of lamb slices, garnished with oregano and roasted garlic bulbs and surrounded by glistening potatoes. Zeno followed with a plate of tomato slices, feta cheese and black olives. They raised their glasses. "Are you Athenian?" Claire asked Mina, who was seated on her left.

"No, Kytherean. I'm Byron's connection to this island. We were visiting my parents in Potamos when we met the Ladases. My parents run the village pharmacy—you know the one, next to the hospital? It's new and—."

"And you have an art gallery?"

"Yes. I spend most of my time there. Byron teaches at the university. Do you see that book over there?" Mina pointed to a thick tome lying open, face-up, on a side table, a plastic-banded wristwatch marking the place. "It's Byron's. He's a philosopher of aesthetics. You know, when he was only five years old—."

"All art is Platonic, though the philosopher himself wouldn't have approved of the idea," Claire overheard Byron say. She remembered having connected Plato's desire to banish art to the faceless icon at the monastery. Vestiges of the East had resided in that great Western mind. She held up a forefinger, indicating to Mina that she would like to hear more of what Byron was saying. "The work of art doesn't change," he continued. "Plato's world of ideas grew out of his belief that knowledge is the supreme virtue and our world can never be truly known because it's in constant flux. And so we have the ideal world, which is fixed. Like art." Claire watched Byron's mouth as he spoke. Sexy, she decided, the upper front teeth very straight and gleaming, but sort of squared off, giving the eye teeth a slight prominence. A little predatory.

"Or daydreams, or our image of the past," Mina volunteered. "Who is that philosopher," she placed a proprietary hand on her husband's arm, "the one who says you can't step into the same river twice?"

"Heraclitus."

"Yes. Well, that's just silly. Of course you can." Mina used her hands for emphasis when she spoke, setting her bracelets jangling. "That is if you take the 'river' to mean the channel through which the water runs and the source of that water. The river isn't the water itself. Word games. And you can 'go home again.' Who said you can't? Look at *me*. Naturally things change. But why don't they just say that?" Claire was beginning to see that underlying Mina's constant chatter was a rather keen, albeit literal, intelligence. "Of course the present Kythera is not the island I knew as a child. That Kythera is fixed in my head, like art. So, tell me, is that the real Kythera, or the one that exists now?"

"Yes. 'How can we know the dancer from the dance?'" Claire put in, thinking of Yeats. Since her return to Greece, fragments of the poetry she hadn't read in years kept coming to mind. Mina took a deep breath through her nose as if she had been holding it through the length of her spiel. It occurred to Claire that she shared with Mina, though to a lesser degree, the return to Kythera in search of something lost.

"Semantics, my dear." Byron patted his wife's plump hand, more to silence her than to explain. "Where would we philosophers be without the ambiguity of language? There would be nothing to talk or write about."

"I've just been admiring our hosts' art," Claire remarked to Byron. "They use a lot of the same colors and shapes, though they have very different styles."

"Yes. I like to show them together in our gallery. Their separate works seem to be part of a single process. They 'speak to one another,' as they say."

"It seems," Zoe said, "as if his works are sort of—explosions of her forms."

Claire thought back to her first marriage and the continual building, or rebuilding, after John's destructive rages. Perhaps there was something in the Ladases' art that told of the male and female principles.

"Yes, Zoe," Byron replied. "Or the reverse. You could say that out of his primal chaos come her forms." His eyes lingered for a while on Zoe's face. Her carved lips, prominent cheekbones, and fiery hair looked particularly lovely in the candlelight. "At any rate, Claire, I wholeheartedly agree. They're wonderful artists. And, I'm happy to say, sell very well."

Noticing that the other guests had almost finished eating, Claire withdrew from the conversation to concentrate on the remaining bits of meat and potatoes on her plate. When Mina turned to ask her why she had come to Kythera, she responded briefly and asked her if she knew Eleni Pappadopoulos.

"No."

"She lives in Kapsali. She and her husband own a café."

"Oh," Mina said, raising her arm. "Eleni Karvouni. Yes, I do. Or did. As schoolgirls. We lived on opposite ends of the island, but I would see her from time to time shopping with her mother in Potamos, or on those rare occasions when we crossed the island to go to the Sempreviva for dinner on a Saturday night. She and—."

"The Sempreviva?"

"A taverna." Mina's expression had changed from one of pleased recognition to a mixture of pity and censure. "Not a good marriage, I'm afraid. Or so I've heard. I always find that so sad. I can't imagine, of course. I've been very, very lucky." She turned an admiring glance at her husband. "How women can find themselves in such—are you—."

"Are you speaking of Eleni Pappadopoulos?" Alex inquired. Mina looked hurt by the interruption.

"Yes. Do you know her, Alex?" Claire asked.

"Of course. Zeno and I go to her café almost every evening to watch the sunset, and she sits for me sometimes. Or did for some preliminary sketches. There's a quality there—I don't quite know how to describe it. Excuse me a moment." Alex, seeing that Zeno had cleared the plates, rose from the table and went to the kitchen. When she returned, she held ceremoniously before her a cake glowing with candles. "Happy Birthday!" everyone cried, looking at Zoe. Claire hadn't known it was Zoe's birthday. Now as she watched her blow out the candles, she understood her friend's insistence that she join them.

Throughout the meal Zoe, who seemed weary, had been talking quietly to the man from Malta. Mina and the conversation that had issued from her remarks had made it impossible for Claire to speak to him, though he was sitting beside her, or to hear anything of his and Zoe's conversation. At any rate, he didn't particularly interest her. The vibrant, articulate Byron overshadowed the small, undistinguished man, who seemed to have little to say. As the group watched Zoe cut the cake, Claire had the chance to observe him. His hands were large and rough like those of a carpenter or a stonemason, and he seemed out of place in that company. There was something strange about his eyes, a watchfulness that brought to mind a fugitive or the victim of some terrible oppression. And he looked familiar. Claire knew she had seen him before, coming or going from Zoe's bungalow she assumed. Then she realized he was passing her a piece of cake.

"Oh, it looks wonderful."

"A syrup cake, *revani*," the Maltese said, seeming as pleased by her response as if he had baked it himself. She noticed that he wasn't having any.

"It's the island cake," Mina announced. "My mother made it. Perhaps you know, Claire, that every island has its own special cake. Ours is made from the bitter almonds grown here. My grandfather had an almond orchard and every year we would—." Claire didn't follow the rest of Mina's story. She was too discomfited by the man from Malta, whose name she couldn't remember, for he was openly staring at her as she ate the cake.

"Where are you from?" Claire asked him, knowing the answer but unable to think of anything else to say. She was unwilling to confess that she had forgotten his name.

"Malta."

"And why are you here?"

"For the caves. I don't like to travel, but I must as part of my job. I explore caves." He had a slightly British accent.

"Oh, you're a spelunker."

"Yes." He seemed distracted by something. "Uh, pardon me, you have a spot—right there." He pointed delicately to a tiny sphere of grease on the front of her white T-shirt. "I just thought you'd want to know so—."

"Oh. Yes, I see. Thank you." Claire felt herself blush.

She was strangely moved by the caver's simple observation of a spot on her clothing. She still didn't know his name. Zoe had slept while

Claire drove home, so she hadn't been able to ask her anything about him. She would the next day, she thought, as she stood at her kitchen sink, vigorously brushing a light bleach-solution on the food spot. She was wide awake, not ready for bed, though it was nearly two in the morning. Her limbs felt warm, fluid and light, as they used to feel after a massage. And yet not the same, for after a massage her mind had been quiet, and now it was racing, inchoate thoughts moving back and forth in her head like trapped insects. All her analytical faculties rushed, like white cells to an infection, to examine the impact of that single, oddly innocent, remark. It had been direct, inappropriate, even intimate. Perhaps it was that, the homely intimacy of the remark, which had so moved her. And her body—yes, "fluid" was the word, as if poised to move effortlessly into some natural and final form, like the sea into the bay of Kapsali. A welcome entropy.

Women are protean, she had read once, shape-shifters. She thought of her daughter and of the metamorphosis of Daphne. She remembered her own contortions to fit the psyches and physiques of the men she had loved, acrobatic transformations, requiring great strength and dexterity, extreme acts of energy and will. This, on the other hand, felt easy, like the downhill road to Myrtidion. And the cause of it all, an awkward, spiderlike man with gray hair and a disproportionately large nose splayed across his face. An unattractive man, who had pointed out a food spot on her clothing.

6

THE NEXT MORNING CLAIRE was awake early but remained in bed, staring at the knots on the pine-panelled ceiling, smiling, still aroused and desperate to know more about the unusual man from Malta. The birds had just started up, and the curtains over the small window on the opposite wall were edged with light. Perhaps she could catch Zoe before she set off to work. She got out of bed and lit the stove for coffee, aware again of how smoothly she seemed to be moving, as though she were suddenly walking through a new and less-resistant element. After spreading marmalade on a couple of rusks, she took them and a mug of coffee to the porch. Looking intently towards Zoe's bungalow, her entire being concentrated there, she waited for a sign that she was awake.

The air was soft and cool but without chill. The sun was just peeping over the hill behind Kapsali, casting an orange light over the forecourt and teasing out the pine sap smell of the trees. She got up to refill her mug and returned to her vigil, readjusting her chair so that it was more squarely facing Zoe's porch. Nothing yet. Finally, she saw some movement, Zoe's front door opening, then Zoe. Claire jumped to her feet and started down the stairs. When she reached the bottom, she looked up and saw it wasn't Zoe. It was a man, in fact. She leaned against the post and watched, waiting for him to leave and amusing herself with the ribbing she planned to give her friend when she realized, with a sharp intake of breath, that the man was Byron Velisarios. He had started across the yard, walking very quickly, head down, and disappeared behind a pine tree. He hadn't seen her. The tryst, from his point of view, had remained private.

Was the act a sin only when perceived by a third party? Was she changing the nature of something by merely observing it? Like

Berkeley's tree falling in the forest—or those experiments she was hearing about where physicists, by merely observing subatomic particles, change their behavior. One thing she did know. She was shaken by the sight and disappointed in her friend. To all but the lovers themselves, the extramarital affair was a paltry thing and certainly ruthless, with much of its excitement hinging on the forbidden element, the betrayal. Even Tristan and Isolde missed the thrill once they were outside the bounds of society, in the freedom of the woods. Claire had lost her enthusiasm for speaking to Zoe about the man from Malta and walked slowly back up the stairs. Though, unlike Byron, she was free to fall in love, she began to question her seemingly endless capacity to do so. She would try to forget the night before. The day was going to be hot. She would shower, pack a little lunch, and return to her cove by the unfinished hotel.

"Claire!" Zoe's voice. She stepped out of the shower, wrapped a towel around herself, and dashed to the door. "Sorry, I'm out of milk for coffee. Have you any?"

Claire went to the tiny fridge, withdrew a carton, and handed it to her.

"*Gala.*" Claire said the Greek word. In the previous weeks, she had mastered most of the food words and found the new naming thing fascinating. It was like breaking up for a second time the seamless, innocent world of infancy. As we named things, they became separated from us, "fallings from us" Wordsworth had written. Was it with language then that the exile from Eden began? Claire would look at a hunk of cheese as if for the first time and try to decide which word better expressed its essence, "cheese" or "*tiri.*" "*Gala*" with the accent on the first syllable seemed far more suggestive of the white grassy-smelling substance from cows and goats than "milk." And it had the added force of seniority. The Greek language had come first, and Greece was a land of first things. It was a place, a famous traveler had remarked, where every donkey seemed "the first donk."

Zoe appeared less tired that morning, and Claire wondered about the root of the previous day's weariness. Some complication with Byron no doubt. The doctor lingered on the porch, clutching the carton of milk against her chest, looking as if she wanted to say something. On the verge of a confession perhaps? Claire hoped not. Zoe said she had the day off, and they made plans to go to the beach together.

There was no breeze, and the water sliding lazily into the tiny inlet made a lovely music, swooshing around the curvature of the rock walls, gurgling into crevices, and whispering as it withdrew from the curve of shingle. They lay contentedly on their straw mats, absorbing the sun's soft, deep heat. On their way down, Claire had noticed Dimitri hunkered on a large rock, nonchalantly tossing pebbles into the waterless swimming pool. Did he come there every day? Or did he have a lookout from which he could see people coming and then proceed to the desolate hotel? Claire opened her eyes and turned to Zoe. "Did you see him when we came down?"

"Who?"

"The voyeur."

"No. Where is he?" Zoe's eyes remained closed.

"He was by the hotel pool. Now he's probably in one of those little cottages above. He can stay hidden there and maintain his view of the beach. Of us, ugh, like Pentheus watching the Bacchae from a tree. He gives me the creeps. I would leave my swimsuit on for spite, but I refuse to let him deprive me of a thorough suntan."

"Hmm." Zoe rolled on her side. Claire could see she took the rotisserie approach to tanning. "'Hell is other people.'"

"What?"

"'Hell is other people.' Some philosopher said that, can't remember who."

"Well, can you remember why he said it? I mean how are other people hell?"

"They make objects of us. You see? It's a kind of death. I remember now—Sartre, that's who said it. Anyway, death is the final objectification,

45

the greatest shame. The voyeur is just an extreme case of—other people. Without other people, there is no shame."

Claire was thinking of what she had just seen that morning. "And what about guilt? Or is there only sin when there's an observer?"

"That's different. Don't forget about God, who is all-seeing, the ultimate voyeur." Zoe cast a wry smile in her friend's direction.

"Oh, yes." Claire laughed and, at the same time, understood that a humanized, personal God, non-existent as far as she was concerned, was, for Zoe, a reality. Suddenly she was too hot and wanted to swim. She lifted the hair off her neck into a clip, walked quickly over the hot uneven surface of the pebbles, and plunged into the cool water. She was almost out to the open sea before she turned on her back to float and let her thoughts wander.

Seeing Byron Velisarios leaving Zoe's bungalow at that telltale time of the morning had brought to mind the suffering she had undergone in her last marriage. Tony also had had a "weakness for the ladies"— that quaint, eye-winking phrase for philanderers. The wink, the half-closed eye, a kind of permission, a way of saying I see but I don't see, so carry on. It had been a painful discovery. She had actually caught him in the act, having set out to catch him, all the while hoping her hunches would prove incorrect. He was employed in his family's wine business and travelled a lot, and there had been something about his demeanor during that period that aroused her suspicions. If he had a flight in the early morning, he would book into an airport hotel the night before. Aware of the opportunity that the practise allowed him, she had gone to the hotel one evening and, announcing herself as his wife, elicited a key from the desk clerk and let herself into his room. It was empty at the time but obviously inhabited by two people. There were unfamiliar objects on one of the bedside tables and, when she opened the door of the closet, she saw a woman's dress and shoes. Her heart racing, she sat down on the bed and smoked a cigarette, after which she left the room, miserable but at least armed with knowledge. The pain had been oddly mitigated by her successful detective work, by suspicions confirmed. When she confronted him on his return, he became enraged and vanished for another few days. Then he reappeared, remorseful, apologetic, even tearful, and protested that it had meant nothing and would never happen again. But, of course, it had.

A year or so later, she found a note on the floor of the entrance hall, under the console table where her husband often emptied his pockets of change. The words "Tues 14, Enrico's—8" were scrawled on a small scrap of paper. Recognizing the restaurant as a local one, she checked her calendar and found that the fourteenth had fallen on a Tuesday the month before, during a week he was presumably in Los Angeles marketing a new wine. Again, the recriminations and tears, the declarations of love and vows to be faithful. It was not long after the second discovery that a good friend of hers, sympathetically silent for years, revealed to her that her husand had always been unfaithful, still was, everyone knew, and so on. Then, in humiliation and rage, and despite her daughter's protestations, Claire ended the marriage.

She swam farther out to sea, doing rapid crawl strokes, floated for a while, and then returned at a more leisurely pace to the cove. Back on the beach again, she watched Zoe splash playfully in the water. She really was a wonderful specimen, Claire thought, admiring the long, perfectly moulded arms and legs, the high firm breasts, the heart-shaped expressive face topped by the black-rooted, fiercely cut red hair.

"What did you think of George Vrilakis?" Zoe shouted over the water music. So that was his name. George. It suited him.

"'Vrilakis' is Greek, isn't it?"

"Yes, but it's several generations back. He's from Malta."

"I know. Tell me about him."

"Well, he's a spelunker."

"I know."

"His project is over in Crete, and he's back and forth a lot. Came here by accident. I mean literally. He was aboard a freighter that caught fire just out there." Zoe, waist high in the water, turned and gestured towards the spot. "There were too many crew and passengers for the few hotels here, so some of the islanders took them in until they could reboard or find another way to Crete. That's how he met the Ladases. They've grown fond of one another."

"Where is he staying?"

"With them."

"Oh, I thought he was just another dinner guest last night, but now I see that he was actually sort of home."

"Right. He'd just been up in the Chora making travel arrangements. He also uses the Ladases' apartment from time to time in Crete. In Chania. That's when he's not at his cave."

"Married?"

"No." Zoe smiled meaningfully. "He left again this morning."

Claire felt a pang of disappointment. Well, that was settled. Better to keep the little fantasy intact, "unheard melodies" and all that.

"But he'll be back," Zoe added, smiling broadly. "That is after he has penetrated the cave a few hundred more metres and some engineers have made it safe for the archaeologists to take over again. Then he can rest until they've thoroughly explored that segment, and so it continues until the end has been reached or the rains begin, whichever comes first. He's been in the area for a few months and may be here a few more."

Claire suppressed the urge to ask how long it might be before he returned to Kythera.

"There he is!" Zoe shouted. Claire turned around, half-expecting to see George. There was no one. She looked quizzically at Zoe. "Our observer," Zoe said. She pointed up to the lower cottage and came out of the water, sleek and dripping. Still looking up, she placed one hand on the black triangle of her naked crotch, undulated slightly, and waved exuberantly with the other. Dimitri was getting quite a show today. Zoe's brash greeting, Claire realized, was her way of solving the subject-object problem, of creating a balance. And it might even drive him away. Not a bad idea if you lacked inhibitions, and easier if there were two of you.

7

A PERKY LITTLE FISHING BOAT, right out of one of Annabel's storybooks, even to its prow pointing skyward like a retroussé nose, was returning to the harbor, followed closely by a flock of ravenous gulls. The boat's motor and the shriek of the birds were the only sounds to be heard. The street was deserted except for a few sleepy-looking merchants, sitting alone outside their shops, having their ritual *kafés*. As Claire walked along, she was aware of the strong vanilla scent of oleander, still blooming in tall clumps along the seawall and throwing long shadows across her path. She had mentioned to Eleni her interest in Greek dishes, asking her for recipes or demonstrations. It was a sincere request and had the added advantage of giving her further entry into the Greek woman's life. Eleni had asked her to come at seven.

Claire turned into the road that she had taken on her first day back in Kythera, the one that angled off from the main street and ran along the inner bay. It was empty at this hour, except for some prowling cats and a couple of geese. The young pepper trees next to the breakwater were now in bright green leaf. Claire knew the house, had been aware of it before she knew it as Eleni's. It was a whitewashed stucco block like the other houses on the road but, unlike the others, hadn't been painted for years. She had admired the exterior's modulations of plaster, the marbling of chalk and ash where the paint had entirely disappeared. The arbored porch, which extended the length of the house, was now a riot of midsummer vegetation with a lush canopy of grape vines and flourishing geraniums spilling over old olive oil cans placed along the edge to catch the sunlight. Eleni sat in a chair by the front door, an orange cat in her lap.

"*Kalispera.*"

"*Kalispera.*"

"*Ella*. Come." Eleni poured the cat from her lap, and Claire followed her into the house. They passed through the small, dark sitting room and into the kitchen. Eleni's husband, a weedy figure in loose trousers and a thin sleeveless undershirt, was sitting at an oilcloth-covered table. Before him on the table were the predictable afternoon *kafés, a* glass of ice water and a dollop of jamlike spoon-sweet. He hadn't looked up when they entered the kitchen. "This is my husband, Aleko." A few minutes lapsed before he rose from the table and, without a word, left the room. "He goes now to play cards," Eleni said, as if to explain her husband's rudeness. On another table, adjacent to the stove, were the ingredients for the island syrup cake: honey, lemons, sugar, a small package of flour with a large number four on its front, almonds, eggs, butter, spices and milk. Claire took the coffee Eleni offered her, pulled out a pen and notebook, and sat down on the chair Aleko had vacated.

Eleni opened the large jar of the local thyme honey. The dark sticky stuff flowed slowly over the lip of the jar into the saucepan. Claire observed the Greek woman as she added water and turned on the burner. Her waist, around which she had tied a bib-type apron, had thickened over the years, and her manner of dress was an odd combination of the girlish and the matronly, the ankle socks, hair band and loose-fitting dress falling to an awkward mid-calf length. It was as if she had missed the important in-between segment, the stage she was made for, nature's female, alluring and fertile. Of course, Eleni was nearly past that, as she would be soon herself, but there were no vestiges even of sexuality. Eleni removed the saucepan from the stove and squeezed a few drops from a lemon into the mixture. "After it's cool," she said, "I add brandy." She crossed to a high cupboard, opened it, and took out a bottle of Metaxa. She moved like the honey, Claire observed, slowly and with a kind of stiffness.

Claire was reminded of the rigidity she had felt in her own limbs and spine until that night at the Ladases' house. She was still feeling the effects of her encounter with the caver, even though she had cautioned herself against impossible romantic dreams and the magician had gone. His words had cast a spell. Claire smiled, remembering them—"you have a spot right there." How absurd, how unlike the words she would have chosen for a fictional seduction.

"It's cool now," Eleni said, putting a forefinger into the syrup. She sucked her finger clean, added the brandy and handed the mixture to Claire, who dipped in a finger and tasted. "Um, delicious!" Claire exclaimed. Eleni blushed and mouthed the new word. "Delicious," she said, smiling and bringing her hand to her mouth. Claire suspected that she had fallen into the habit as a way of hiding her slightly protruding teeth, which were not unattractive. She estimated the amounts Eleni had put into the syrup and wrote them down. She could experiment with American measures when she got back.

The fleeting thought of home took her by surprise. She felt a rush of longing as she pictured Annabel with her tiny arms raised, asking to be picked up. Since her arrival, Claire had thought little of the inevitable return, and she dismissed the thought now in order to concentrate on the process at hand. After the butter had softened, Eleni cracked three eggs, deftly separating the yolks from the whites. She was a graceful cook. She added the sugar and egg yolks to the butter and, with wide rapid strokes, beat the mixture.

"Do you like Athens?" Claire asked. It was always an amusing question to ask the locals, for it was usually met with raised eyebrows, an emphatic downturning of the mouth, and myriad gestures suggesting noise, bad smells and confusion.

"*Then ksero.*"

"You don't know?"

"I don't go."

"Do you mean you have never gone?"

"No. I don't go from Kythera."

"To Crete?"

"*Oxi.* No place." Eleni had been sifting the flour and spices and was adding them to the butter mixture alternately with the milk. "Remember, this is number-four flour. Very important." Claire recalled all the different flours in the Greek shops and wondered which was the closest to the common white flour she was used to. She crossed to the worktable, reached into the flour package for a sample, and rubbed the grain between her fingers, trying to recall the texture of the American product.

"You've never been off this island," she said to the Eleni, interrupting her vigorous beating of the egg whites. Eleni put down her whisk and copper bowl and wiped her hands on her apron.

"*Ella*," she said, and gestured for Claire to follow. They walked through the sitting room to the front porch. This time through, Claire noticed the needlework, crocheted afghans on the settee, lace doilies and embroidered squares on the tables. A Greek woman's dowry. Eleni shooed a stray cat from the porch and took Claire's hand. Together they descended the steps to the street. "Look." Eleni pointed towards the flaming red disk in the western sky that would soon sink behind the old fortress. Then she raised her arm to the east where the other orb, white and sheer as organdy, was on the rise. "You see. Everything is here."

Claire was moved by her words and by something else as well. As Eleni raised her arm to the moon, she saw the unfinished painting in the Ladases' studio. She remembered Alex's saying that Eleni had sat for her. The profile was identical. Of course. The artist had used her for the Daphne figure. Eleni had been a muse for Alex as well.

"Now, we finish the cake," Eleni announced, turning back towards the house. She brought the cat inside, and they returned to the kitchen.

Claire retraced her steps down the strand, just then beginning to come alive. As she passed the café, Eleni's mother, a kerchiefed and aproned sphere of black cloth, was setting tables, and Aleko was already perched at his station inside behind the cash register. Claire saw Alex and Zeno Ladas, the evening's first customers, sitting by the seawall. She was delighted when Alex hailed her, motioning her to join them. They were charming people, and their mysterious long-term house guest hardly lessened their appeal. Almost a week had passed since the birthday party. Zeno stood up and pulled out a chair.

The waiter approached, and Claire ordered a small bottle of retsina. The alternative to the typical 750 ml bottle was a small soda-type one with a metal cap. "I've been visiting Eleni. Or maybe I should say 'Daphne.'"

"You noticed," she replied.

"Yes, and I understand. There is something rooted about her. It's enviable, her life, its innocence and continuity. Like the rocks around here. She seems to have—there's a phrase, 'unity of being.' She has that."

"She has never been off the island," Zeno said, pouring water into his ouzo. He asked the waiter who had brought Claire's retsina for some *meze*.

"That's part of it, I suppose. One wonders what that must be like. But I think that's why she seems so complete. She told me tonight that everything is here."

"Everything that matters, anyway," Zeno said, standing up. "I see a boat's just come in. I'm going to try to buy a fish."

"But then," Alex protested, "everything isn't here, really. Not even, as Zeno says, everything that 'matters.' And how can she truly appreciate the beauty of this island when she's never seen anything else?"

The waiter repositioned the ouzo bottle and placed two small plates on the table, *dolmas* and a small block of feta.

"I've thought that too," Claire said, becoming aware of a cat slinking around the table legs. She picked up a fork from a plastic basket of utensils and stabbed a rice-filled grape leaf, at the same time nudging the cat away with her foot. "She's so at one with this place, like these cats really. She can't possibly *see* it. And I would imagine that most of the islanders have at least been to Athens."

"It is puzzling," Alex said. "But remember Daphne didn't choose to become a tree, freely that is."

"Hmm. Have you finished it?" Claire pulled a Papastrato from a fresh pack, offering one to Alex, who declined. She hadn't remembered seeing her smoke. Fewer people did now—even artists, even here. She enjoyed smoking, and it was, for her, a perverse act of freedom, like that of the man in the Russian novel who believes he has a diseased liver and refuses to see a doctor. Novels. Alex had given her an idea. There might be some pathology behind Eleni's never having left the island.

"I've painted very little this week," Alex replied, gathering another feral cat into her lap and petting it with long, eager strokes. "We were busy for a while with Byron and Mina, and there've been other things having to do with the Crete gallery. Life intrudes. But we're exhibiting in Potamos soon, and I want to have the 'Daphne' finished. Oh, here's Zeno. And with a fish. He's obsessed with fish! I suppose we must go now." Alex stood up, and she and Claire embraced.

After the couple departed, Claire finished her cigarette and a second glass of wine. She hadn't asked them anything about George. It seemed a point of honor not to use them in that way. Zoe was different, for single women together were natural conspirators. The passing of that sort of information was understood, even expected. The rich smell of eggplant frying in olive oil wafted through the air. A large local family and a young German couple had sat down. The sky to the west was sprinkled with a few stars, and it was at its most intense blue, the last blue before the dark. Claire gazed out over the water, then as black as the face of the madonna in the icon. Empty and therefore infinite in its possibilities.

Eleni carefully lowered the container of warm goat's milk into the earth and, with another rope, drew up a bucket of water. She tipped the contents of the bucket into an urn and then, hoisting it on her shoulder, walked back across the garden, around the lines where their bedsheets snapped like sails in the breeze, and into the house. That summer Serena had been fascinated by the well, for, as she boasted to Eleni, everyone in Australia had plumbing and big white electric boxes called "refrigerators."

Eleni had learned about refrigerators in science class because they operated on an important law of nature, the one that says that heat flows from a hotter body to a colder body until both are the same temperature unless energy is applied, and that was where refrigerators came in. She had found the lesson intriguing, particularly when the teacher pointed out that the future merging of temperatures in space meant the heat death of the universe. He called the state of separation, whether it was separate temperatures or something else that might later be mixed, like wine and water, "order," the uniform or mixed state "disorder." Eleni found that strange. She thought about lovers, one warm, the other cold, embracing on a winter's night and becoming the same temperature, living together for decades and becoming the same person. Love. How could that be called "disorder"? Or even if the earth were to burn up and become one with the rest of the universe, wasn't that being with God? Wasn't that what everyone was supposed to pray for? How could that be called "disorder"?

She had learned lots of things about the world, not only from school, but from her cousin as well. It was Serena, for instance, who had prepared her for the previous year's sudden show of blood on her underpants, bright as the poppies in spring. She remembered that day two years ago in June, the morning after Serena had arrived for the summer. The cousins had taken one of the Karvounis' goats on a leud down the main road of Kalamos and into an open field, which fanned out and down to become the hills above Kapsali. The field was alive with the moving colors of wildflowers in the breeze. Eleni and Serena tied the goat to the trunk of an oak tree and found a flat outcropping of rock on which to sit among a delightful profusion of poppies, daisies, dandelions and broom. Far below, the only man-made thing in sight was a tiny church and walled graveyard lined with cypress trees, whose fixed dark verticality anchored the breeze-softened pastoral. Eleni's mother had told her that the vertical cypresses were male and the more prostrate female (the closest Tula had ever come to a discussion of sex), but she had been wrong. Eleni had learned in botany that each type of cypress possessed both male and female. And she also knew that they were symbols of the resurrection, but also of the phallus. It was very confusing, all these opposites, separateness and oneness, God and genitalia. She suspected the problem might be with the words themselves.

Eleni pulled from her pocket two pieces of the anise-flavored candy she had saved and handed one to her cousin. Then she told Serena about the Italian fishermen. It had been many weeks since she had seen them. One Tuesday they simply hadn't come. The next Tuesday Eleni still had her mother do her hair in the elaborate style, but again they had not appeared. The following week she wore her braids down but still hoped, and by the next she had given up. Or, if she hadn't exactly given up, she was no longer going to Kapsali early on Tuesdays chasing the idea of Carlo. She had saved the candy as proof of their meetings, a kind of souvenir and way of reliving the experience. As they sat on the rock sucking the hard candy, Serena, a year older than her cousin, told Eleni the facts about love, men and women and what they did. She also explained menstruation, dramatizing the biological description she had received in school with her own experience of pain and inconvenience.

The monthly time had come around again, and Eleni felt a twinge as she placed the heavy urn on the marble slab just inside the kitchen door. The cramp would become increasingly painful, radiating down and deep into her thighs, a strong stubborn tug like the old well drawing the milk into its depths. It was Saturday, the day Eleni and Tula prepared Sunday's dinner, to which they would invite relatives and friends, and sometimes the priest.

Tula was already melting butter and rolling out sheets of filo dough. Eleni dragged a small chair to the oilcloth-covered table, over which hung, like an icon, the large and ornately framed photograph of her father taken in Athens two years before his death. Eleni had been an infant when he died, so she had no memory of him. Her mother had told her that in the early days of their marriage they had often gone to Athens and stayed with her brother-in-law and his wife. She frequently fell into a reminiscence, recounting the happy, spirited holidays they had spent there. Eleni sat down and reached for the bowl of walnuts to shell. She enjoyed the task, the sound of the loud hollow crack as the hammer broke the shell and, though she would finally chop the nuts, the challenge of digging out each lobe of the nutmeat intact.

After the baklava was assembled, they began the tomatoes. Eleni, still at the table, scooped out the juicy red flesh from the skins while her mother stood at the stove sautéing chopped onions with oregano and the bit of ground lamb she had purchased that morning from the butcher in the Chora. She mixed the tomato pulp and juices with cooked rice and added the meat mixture along with mint and a dash of cinnamon. Mother and daughter together stuffed the tomatoes, carefully replacing their green-stemmed caps. They thought the dish looked even more beautiful than usual, for it represented the last of the tomatoes from their garden. Then they carried the pans to the baker in the village. Every Saturday they prepared the Sunday meal, and every Saturday night their efforts were rewarded by an evening out at the taverna.

The Sempreviva was a tradition on that end of the island. It was a long stucco block, its bluntness unrelieved by climbing vines or surrounding trees, sitting as it did on an elevated expanse exposed to the strong island winds. The taverna had been painted an ochre color, and its name stretched across the length of it in large red letters. It was leased by a local farmer and was open only on Saturday nights. The farmer would slaughter a lamb or pig, and his wife would prepare appetizers, vegetables and desserts. Their older daughter, a friend of Eleni's, set the tables, and she and her mother together greeted and waited on customers. A younger sister and brother stood by to fetch extra plates or utensils and clear the tables as the courses progressed. The diners were the same every Saturday—many of the residents of Kalamos, mostly farmers and their families, as well as some families from nearby Kapsali and the Chora. Now and then people from more distant parts of the island would appear, but usually as guests of the regulars.

That night Eleni, her mother and grandfather took a table near the kitchen for the added warmth it would provide. It was only September, but the nights were getting cooler. Eleni's friend gradually filled the table with food—the yoghurt garlic spread Eleni loved, cheese pies, a plate of greens with wedges of lemon, and bread. The room was strongly lit, the excessive brightness a proud display of the recent addition of electricity, still expensive and therefore scarce on the island. Eleni looked around for Kosta and found him sitting as usual with his aunt, uncle and cousin. She rarely saw him except on these Saturday nights because he was no longer in school. She patted the top of her head, making certain that her braids were still in place, and played with the beads of her necklace.

After Carlo disappeared, Eleni had eliminated every boy her age as a desirable mate, except for Kosta, who was in love with Pelagia. She had seen her rival on entering the taverna, her beautiful face outshining even the light the new electricity provided. Eleni was realistic enough to know that she could never hope to take Pelagia's place in Kosta's heart, but she thought that if one Saturday night Pelagia did not come to the taverna, she would at least have an opportunity to talk to him. If they talked, she felt, she might become his friend or "confidante," that word Serena had used. And then it wasn't too far-fetched to imagine Pelagia gone. Kosta, needing consolation for Pelagia's absence and finding its most comforting form in Eleni, would begin perhaps to love her. (Eleni's daydreams had grown a little sinister— Pelagia "gone"as in moved away, to the mainland perhaps, or as in "dead." She had come to realize how what they called "profane" love—although it felt sacred—inspired evil and had even confessed her daydream to the priest.)

These things happened she knew. She read novels with beautiful women and handsome men on the covers, and she saw American movies in the summertime on a large screen set up in the vacant lot between the taverna and hardware store in Livadi. But nothing would happen with Kosta that night. And there, looking in her direction, was Aleko, whom she despised. She dipped her bread deep into the garlic spread, hoping her breath might keep him away.

After the meal came the music and dancing. To begin, everyone joined hands to make a circle, the designated leader and person next to him each holding one end of a handkerchief. When the leader let go of it, breaking the circle, he took the line of dancers into another circle within the first, and so on until everyone was in a coil. Then the partner, now the last in line, moved in the opposite direction to unravel the ball. Aleko had managed, as usual, to grab Eleni's hand for the dance, even though he was on the other side of the room when the music began. Their mothers were good friends, and they found Aleko's eagerness amusing. Once Eleni had overheard them at the baker's joking about some day sharing the same grandchildren.

Eleni hated the way she felt when Aleko's cool wet hand held hers. That night, as the circle for the Labyrinth had begun to form, he touched her other places as well— her waist, her back, her side very near her breasts. He acted as if the contacts were accidental, and he never met her eyes. When the evening was over and Eleni was home and lighting the string in the saucer of olive oil for her nightlight, she remembered the way hers and Carlo's eyes had met. She knew that if Aleko ever looked at her as the fisherman had, she would, like Daphne in the myth, leaf out and become a tree.

8

CLAIRE CARRIED TWO STRING BAGS heavy with produce up the stairs to her bungalow, and Yiannis followed with another bag and a carton of bottled water. It was still only nine o'clock. She had decided to do her Sunday marketing early before it got too hot and the cruise ship arrived to disgorge its masses of people into the village and its shops. She thought of the mindless passivity of the passengers, being carried here and there, emptied out, told when to disembark, when to board. It was like that with all modes of transportation, but the dimming, stupefying effect seemed worse on ships, perhaps because they moved slowly and the journeys were long.

She had made a row of fat red tomatoes on the little counter which separated the kitchen from the sitting room. "*Aromata kai khromata!*" Smell and color, the fruit and vegetable vendors had cried. Appreciating the effect of the tomatoes, she wondered if Thiebaud had ever painted them, as he had rows of lipsticks, high heels and pies. She put the green peppers, eggplants and zucchini in the refrigerator and, taking a straw basket from a shelf, created another still life with the onions and garlic bulbs. Later, she would put together a large ratatouille that would last a while, getting better every day for a few days. Then she would add vinegar, currants, capers, and a bit of sugar to the dish for a caponata. She hung the string bags on a wall hook, stashed the plastic ones under the sink and looked at her watch.

If she hurried, she could be down at the cove by ten. For the next month or two, before it got cool, she wanted to take advantage of every good beach day. Time at the cove had become for her a requirement. The exercise of walking, climbing and swimming was physically therapeutic, and being in such a naturally beautiful place refreshed her spirit. The little beach had an almost hypnotic effect on her in the sense that when she wasn't there, all she had to do was imagine it to duplicate the peace she felt when she was.

On the weekends Zoe often went with her, but the doctor had gone to Athens the day before. Still, with Dimitri lurking about, Claire was seldom alone, and she had reconciled herself to his presence, even to finding the bizarre and silent partnership somewhat comforting. He had become part of the experience of the cove. She never actually looked for him. Sometimes she saw him, and when she didn't, she simply assumed he was there. Claire rarely saw him anywhere else, although that particular morning she had spotted him in town with his brother, a fisherman, whom he sometimes accompanied on his lobster runs. They had looked as if they were gathering provisions for an expedition. Maybe he wouldn't be above the cove today. Would she miss him? Perhaps his spying on her gave her a sense of herself she wouldn't otherwise have. How did that fit in with Zoe's "other people are hell"? Without the voyeur, she thought, she might somehow lose herself in the peaceful womb-like cove, become reimmersed in amniotic waters, become unborn.

The day was still and hot and the water beyond the inlet gray satin. From where Claire sat on her mat, she could see the white prow of another anchored cruise ship. It looked even more enormous from there, magnified by the narrow canvas of sea and sky between the high cliff walls. Then she saw a rhythmic splashing coming towards the beach. Damn it, she said aloud, putting on her swimsuit. Usually if tourists got all the way to the cove, it was by pedalboat.

Claire lit a cigarette and defensively wrapped her arms around her knees, making herself small. She frowned and rapidly puffed away on the Papastrato, as though daring the swimmer to come ashore. As the splashing came closer, she realized the swimmer was male and felt vaguely threatened. She even looked up towards the empty cottages, hoping to catch sight of the voyeur. In shallow water, the swimmer stood upright and scrambled clumsily up the steep shelf of shingle. It was always an awkward ascent, requiring at times all fours, especially when the water was turbulent. The man was small and brown, and, as he stepped up to the beach, she realized it was George Vrilakis. He was grinning widely, not at all apologetic, as if she should be as delighted by the intrusion as he obviously was to find her there. She felt a rush of emotions: surprise because she had thought he was in Crete, confusion at the unannounced interruption of her privacy, and elation that he was there, in the flesh, the man whom she had not stopped thinking about since their first meeting. All those emotions were tinged with a nagging sense of *déjà vu* she could not identify. Not knowing what else to do, she handed him her towel. "Maybe you—."

"No, thank you." He handed it back to her. "May I sit for a while. I've been swimming." She smiled at the obviousness of the remark and buried the butt of the cigarette she had been smoking under some pebbles. She lit a fresh one. George was looking at her, smiling.

"Oh, sorry. Would you like one?" She offered the pack.

"No, thank you," he said, still smiling.

"I thought you were in Crete."

"Oh?"

"Zoe said—."

"Oh, yes, I was going Monday, the day after the birthday party. But Olympic had cancelled all the inter-island flights because of a strike. When I called the project in Crete to tell them I was delayed, I found out that they didn't need me yet anyway. They'd discovered something interesting, and it might be a few more weeks."

"And all this time—."

"Pardon?"

"Oh, nothing. I just thought you were gone, that's all. It's strange to think that and—be wrong." Claire realized, too late, the trace of confession in her remark. She remembered she had been with the Ladases, but then why should they mention that he was still around? "Have you been to this beach before?"

"No."

"But today—."

"I was told you might be here."

"And that's why you came?"

"Yes."

"I thought you might be one of those pesty cruise people," Claire said.

George was resting back against his forearms, legs stretched out and crossed. He looked remarkably comfortable for someone lying on pebbles. He also hadn't responded to her remark. If anything, as he looked out to sea and the prow of the boat, he seemed saddened by something.

She prattled on. "I find them so annoying. They weren't here twenty years ago, you know."

George frowned slightly, and again she had the feeling of not knowing quite what to say to him. She lay back and closed her eyes against the sun.

Several minutes passed, and she heard George in the water. Thinking he might be leaving, she sat up and saw that he was playing in the shallows, floating in a dish shape with only his head and feet above the surface of the water. He tilted his head towards her, smiled a silly smile, and wiggled his toes in greeting. Claire was gratified he wasn't leaving, and she watched him, content to be doing just that and nothing else. He waded out of the water, gleaming. The sun and water, of course, but something else. Suddenly, it struck her where she had seen him before the Ladases' party, and she understood the paramnesia she had had when he stepped upon the beach. George was the man she had seen coming out of the sea on her first day back in Kythera.

As she got up to move her mat closer to the rock wall for some shade, she noticed Dimitri at his station. He wasn't on a fishing expedition after all. George had come out of the water and sat down again. With his hair slicked back, he looked Arabic. He had Arabic blood, she suspected, along with the Greek. "May I ask you something?"

"Of course. Anything." He was staring at her again.

"About a month ago—in fact it was the day I arrived, I was sitting at a café in Kapsali, and I saw a man wade fully dressed out of the water. I think it was you."

"It was."

"But why?"

"Oh." He looked out to the water, lips compressed. There was a brief silence. "I had climbed down to that strip of rock between here and Kapsali. It's not an actual beach and is rather difficult to get to, but there's a small cave there I'd been told about, and I was curious. I think I told you I explore caves." He looked at Claire as if trying to gauge her reaction, not only to his story, but to his vocation. "Well, I was fairly deep in the cave when the tide came up. I had to leave my torch behind and swim back."

"How interesting. There's always a reasonable explanation, isn't there?" Claire picked up her bottle of sunscreen and applied some to her legs, which were, in spite of her new location, still in the sun. "By the way, did you know we're being watched?" She felt she should tell George of Dimitri's presence. Not to tell him seemed a kind of collusion, would make her almost a party to the voyeurism. George glanced up at the cottages and chuckled.

"Have you ever heard the Bushman greeting?" he asked. "One man steps into a clearing and approaches another, who's still hidden behind tall grass. He says, 'I see you.' The second one replies, 'I am here, I see you.' The first responds, 'I am here.'"

Claire laughed. "The original version, I guess, of 'How are you? I'm fine, thank you. And you?' and so on. Purists complain about this, don't they? They say people don't really care how you are and want neither an honest nor a lengthy answer. But that's not the point, is it? It's simply a convention of recognition, important to our sense of identity."

"Of course."

"But Dimitri—that's his name by the way—unlike the Bushman, stays hidden and seeing." Claire gestured towards the cottages and then lay back again and closed her eyes. "Nor does he see us as individuals. A voyeur looks for the generic, I guess—the essential male or female."

"Excuse me." George's standing shadow spread over her, and she opened her eyes. "I just wanted you to know I'm going up there." He pointed to a ledge not too high in the rock face and large enough to sit on. Claire waved a silent goodbye and closed her eyes again, soon falling into a light sleep. When she opened her eyes, she saw George coming down from his niche in the cliff wall. He had something in his hand. "For you," he declared, bowing and handing her a bright yellow flower, one of those she had seen growing out of rock.

"Oh, thank you. I've been meaning to ask someone for the name."

"It's a sempreviva, 'everlasting.' It can live without water, you see."

She examined the little flower, its sturdy stem, the intricacy of its tight petal structure. "Things are often known for what they can do without," he added. Then Claire realized that the taverna where Mina and Eleni had gone in their youth had been named for this indigenous flower. She had passed it many times, a derelict building on the road between Kalamos and Livadi.

George stood at the edge of the water with the look of someone about to plunge. "I've got to get back," he said. "But tomorrow I'd like to take you to a cave. It's a few miles beyond Kapsali, towards Kalamos. A good walk. Will you come?" His back was to her.

"Yes. I'd like that very much."

He turned to her and smiled. "I'll be at the bungalows at ten," he said and slid into the water. He swam with long, energetic strokes towards the mouth of the inlet. Claire watched until she could no longer distinguish him from the blinks of the sun's sparkle on the water.

As Claire turned into the little enclave of bungalows, Zoe was on her way out, walking purposefully, looking lovely in slim blue jeans and a white visor cap. Claire was happy to see her and also surprised, for it was only three o'clock, and the later flight, which Zoe had planned to take, came in from Athens around five. Then she noticed that her friend was in tears.

"God, Claire, I'm glad you're back."

Claire felt the blood drain from her face. Could there have been a message from California? Zoe saw Claire's stricken expression and said hastily, "Oh, no, not a death or anything. And nothing to do with you. Will you walk up to the Chora with me?"

"Not right now, Zoe. I need a shower." By that time Claire had guessed it had to do with Byron Velisarios. "Come to my place. I'll make you a nice drink, and you can wait while I get ready. Then, if you want, we'll go somewhere. Anywhere you like." Zoe followed her to her bungalow and up the steps.

"There now," Claire said, plumping a cushion. "Would you like something?" She marched to the kitchen and pulled open the tiny door of the refrigerator. "I can start water for coffee, or I have—let's see, wine, orange juice…oh, even a can of Coke."

"Coffee, I think. Just put the water on, and I'll do the rest."

When Claire emerged from the bathroom, Zoe, coffee mug in hand, was pacing the small room. "Do you want to tell me about it now, or do you want to go somewhere?"

Zoe stood up, unzipped the nylon pack strapped around her waist, drew out a tissue and blew her nose. "Let's go. I can't sit still. I feel that if I walk quickly enough, I might be able to shake it off."

Almost at the Chora, Zoe decided she had had enough, and they climbed the steps to an outdoor bar-café. It was uniquely situated on a narrow protrusion of high, pine-studded ground, below which the road made a sharp bend, the last bend before the Chora. Tables were set up among the trees, in front and behind the bar. They chose a table in front where they could look down to the water. It was a very pleasant place if one didn't mind the cars going by. They were the only customers, and a boy, who couldn't have been more than twelve years old, brought them iced coffees and a pack of Marlboros. He and a younger girl, probably his sister, stood behind the bar and quietly watched them. Claire pulled some drachmas and a Bic lighter from her shorts pocket, lit Zoe's cigarette and then her own. "Now."

"I—I don't know how to begin."

"Would it help if I told you I saw Byron Velisarios leaving your bungalow early one morning?"

"Ah," Zoe gasped. Her neck became rosy. "You *know*. Well, that does help things along." She reached into her pack for another tissue and blew her nose. "They were friends of mine before, Byron and Mina. I mean before I came here. Did you know that?"

"I had no idea." Beneath them a donkey, on which an old woman rode side-saddle, holding a bunch of leafy beets, lumbered slowly up the hill. Was it patronizing, Claire wondered, to assume that the woman on the donkey had never had such problems? Nor Eleni Pappadopoulos? She looked back to her friend, who seemed to have rallied a bit in the telling of her story. Confessions were a good thing. "How did you know them?"

"Well, when I started at the University of Athens I wanted to study art history. After a year or so, I decided to become a physician and switched to biology. But by that time I'd taken an aesthetics class from Byron and had developed a crush on him. Although I was no longer a student of his, I would see him from time to time in the halls, on the campus grounds— you know.

"Well, one day he stopped and invited me to lunch at his house with some other students and professors. On that day, a Sunday, I met Mina and their children, Myrto and Costas. I found his wife and his children, their house, their art, their little rose garden—the whole set-up—enchanting. Mina asked me if I'd be interested in looking after their children from time to time, and I agreed. I knew I could use the extra money and the idea of having a closer connection to that lovely household appealed to me.

"In a year's time I'd become almost indispensable to them, and when my roommate moved out and I could no longer afford my flat, they invited me to live with them, board and room in exchange for babysitting and helping Mina with household chores. I became a part of the family. I adored little Myrto and Costas, and I liked Mina very much. I shared with her not only the housework but pleasures as well. We became friends. And yet I fell more and more in love with Byron and sensed that the feeling was mutual. But it remained unspoken. There wasn't a single word. Not a single declaration or even a proposition!"

Claire recalled her impression of Byron as the type who would have taken the first opportunity and realized she had not given him enough credit. The number of cars going to and from the Chora was increasing, but the two women were still the only customers in the café. The boy waiter and the girl were now tossing an orange back and forth in front of the bar.

"Then everything changed. I was accepted at med school and left for San Francisco. In my first year there, I had a brief affair with a fellow student, a rebound thing, but that and the enormous academic pressure served to put a wedge between me and my memory of Byron. My only contact with the Velisarios family when I was in California was cards to the children, birthday cards and picture postcards. By the time I returned to Athens, I was over Byron and vowed not to get in touch with them. And then there they were, suddenly at the Ladases' house, right after I arrived in Kythera! Naturally Mina was puzzled and even a little angry that I hadn't contacted them on my return.

"That morning when you saw Byron leave my bungalow was our first time together! All that time under the same roof and nothing, and then the other night—well, definitely something. I think it had more to do with the remarkable coincidence than anything else. It was as if, in spite of all our efforts to be good, it was somehow meant to be. As if we weren't in charge at all. It took on a kind of inevitability. And now—!"

"What?" Now, Claire thought, she would hear the real reason for the tears.

"They're going away—to France for a year! Byron has a sabbatical." Zoe began to cry again.

"But that's so much better, don't you see? You will get over him again!"

"I know. Can we go home now? I'm exhausted." Zoe took a deep breath, sighed, and then stood up resolutely.

About halfway down the hill Zoe suddenly stopped in her tracks. "How stupid of me—I forgot! Looking down at the harbor just reminded me. I was supposed to ask you to join the Ladases and me for dinner tonight. They have a visitor, an Englishman. I'm just not up to it, but I can't call them because they're in Potamos all day. Can you go?" Claire nodded assent. "It's the Pharos, the new restaurant opening down on the pier. Eight o'clock."

As the friends parted at the bungalows, Claire repeated her promise to join the Ladases for dinner and extend Zoe's apologies. Then she sat on her porch for a while before going inside, gazing through the pine branches down to the bay, to the very spot where she had seen George emerge from the water in street clothes. She smiled. She hadn't thought of him since coming across Zoe, and thinking of him now raised her spirits—immeasurably.

Claire was aware of larger crowds in the bars and tavernas as she walked along the bay that evening. It was almost the first of August. In that month, she knew, hundreds of people from the mainland would arrive for festivals all around the island. There were festivals for wine, oranges, figs and almonds, for the patron saints of various villages, for the madonna in all her guises on the fifteenth, the Feast of the Assumption, and for the particular Madonna of the Myrtle, the one with the haunting black face, on the twenty-fourth. Food and religion. Hotel rooms and monastery cells were fully booked. People would be there for prayer, for pleasure, for meditation and merrymaking. Motorcycles and cars would stream all over the island, villages would vibrate nightly with music and dance, the dog-day cicadas would be in full throb.

She spotted the Ladases as soon as she reached the pier. Zeno, with his mane of white hair, stood out from the crowd at the end of the long cement jetty. Their table was one of several against the restaurant's exterior wall. Alex introduced her to their friend, Harry Smythe, and, as she poured wine into Claire's glass, told her that he was a writer of books she didn't understand. They looked at the menu and agreed on a large order of calamari. It was the existence of a menu, Claire surmised, that distinguished the "restaurant" and some "cafés" from the "taverna," where the selection was always given orally, often accompanied by a trip to the kitchen and a peek under pot lids.

Claire turned to Alex. "Zoe can't be here this evening. You weren't home today, so she couldn't phone you. She's very sorry. She had been in Athens and returned early because she didn't feel well."

"Hmm." Alex nodded, knowingly. Claire wondered if the artist had some knowledge of Zoe's problem. "Did you know Mina and Byron are going to France?" Now Claire was certain that Alex, on some level, was aware of Zoe's romantic attachment to Byron.

The calamari arrived, and Claire began to pick at it. She was more tired than hungry and hoped to leave early, desiring a good night's sleep before her walk with George the next morning. She put down her fork, took a sip of wine, and addressed Harry. "What do you write?" She liked the company of other writers, and it had been a while.

"Anything I can! Book reviews, art criticism, magazine articles about how to find a girl, how to train your dog, lose weight, grow asparagus. Anything to support my bad habit, which is writing fiction." Claire liked the fact he didn't seem to take himself too seriously. "And you. What do you write? I've been told you have the same affliction."

"Yes, the fiction affliction. And I write about things I *don't* know—contrary to the usual advice. It's an exploration. Does that make any sense?" Harry nodded, smiling as if he understood. He then turned to Zeno, who was trying to get his attention.

A fishing boat had come in, and two men sat near the edge of the jetty with their legs spread out before them, like children playing a game of jacks. They rapidly picked through a bright yellow net, plucking out pink and brown fishes and tossing them into a growing pile. Zeno wandered over to watch. Harry was watching Zeno and chuckling to himself, giving Claire a chance to observe the observer. In his mid-to-late-thirties, she guessed, tall with a slim, unmuscular physique and a cherubic face, saved from being too pretty by its constant expression of ironic amusement. His fine brown hair was a little longish. Not bad, Claire thought. Rather charming, in fact. Maybe good medicine for Zoe.

"When you're with Zeno, you never go home fishless!" Harry shrieked with laughter as Zeno made his way back to the table, squeamishly holding away from him a jumping paper bag with a still-struggling fish.

"Oh, cruel—kill it," Alex pleaded.

"How do you know the Ladases?" Claire asked Harry.

"I was down here last summer with a friend of mine, a painter, who's also a friend of theirs. The Ladases, you know, lived in London for a while. In fact, I've brought some of our friend's paintings to hang at the Potamos art fair. Chris had to be in Amsterdam, so I'm the courier. I was delighted to have an excuse to return to this place. Enchanting, isn't it?"

"Yes. It puts me in a kind of trance. The air is narcotic. And the light—no wonder artists love it." She rose from the table and reached into her bag for drachmas. "I guess you know George Vrilakis?"

"Yes. Decent chap. In fact, we're sharing a room at the Ladases'. He'd be here tonight, but he's working on a map of the cave he's exploring."

Claire had never thought of a cave map and tried to picture what one would look like. "Well, excuse me, I must be off," she said, putting the appropriate amount on the table. Zeno and Harry stood up. "See you next week at the fair, if not before."

"Oh, absolutely," Harry replied.

The waterfront looked festive. Lights were strung along the seawall, separating the lively scene from the darkness beyond and dividing one crowded pavilion from another. Brightly lit souvenir shops remained open, and music and laughter floated from the open doors of bars into the street. The street itself, from which cars had been prohibited, had become a promenade for young adults, swaggering adolescents, and families with babies in strollers and older children charging ahead on

71

bright little bikes. Greek children, Claire had noticed, never seemed to go to bed. A large gibbous moon, low and red, hung above the hills behind the village. Claire saw Eleni standing against the wall of her café. She seemed to be staring beyond the parade of people, beyond her customers dining next to the seawall, into the dark. "Eleni!" Claire called and waved. The Greek woman started, saw her and smiled, automatically raising her hand to her mouth.

9

"IT'S A CHURCH." CLAIRE STEPPED across the rocky floor of the narrow riverbed and up the small incline of oleander to the large sloped mouth of the cave. Some of it had been painted white, a cross on the rock face just above the mouth, a low-walled area at the entrance that held the iconstasis, candles and offertory box, and the back wall of the first chamber on which hung a series of icons. The white surfaces were brilliant against the dark, dank limestone and black cavity that led farther into the cave.

"It's a holy place, yes. The first churches were caves," George said, dropping from his shoulders the leather straps of a wicker hamper. He placed it on a low table of rock under a pink oleander just outside the entrance.

"I should have thought of that. It occurred to me in the chapel of a monastery recently that churches resemble caves. Not just the cool darkness of some of them, but the decoration too—the stalactites and stalagmites sort of echoed in silver and brass."

"That's true. Even the censers look like helictite, one of the more bizarre formations."

And candles were essential, Claire realized then, at all times, even during the day. Only later, perhaps, would they become symbolic. She was moving along the back wall, from one saint to another, looking at the deeply shadowed Levantine faces and breathing in the ancient dampness of the rock. She turned to George. "Wasn't Zeus supposed to have been born in a cave? In Crete, they say."

"And Jesus, too, but not in Crete of course. There's even a hymn in the Greek liturgy, 'I Parthenos Simeron.' Today the virgin comes to the cave—*spileon* in Greek—to give birth."

Weary from the hot walk, Claire sat down on the cave floor, her back against the wall. "They're sort of cosy, don't you think? I remember as a child spreading a blanket over a table and crawling inside. Did you ever do that? Or after going to bed at night, especially on summer nights when it was still light, making a tiny dim cavern with my bedsheet and mentally putting myself in it. The womb, they say."

"Well, most caves aren't like this," George said, studying one of the icons.

"Do you happen to know where it goes?" Claire looked warily at the forbidding dark cavity that led deeper into the cave.

"Yes. There are just two more chambers. It might have been man-made, it's so accommodating. Flat and small…are you hungry?"

"Very." George moved out towards the basket of food. Claire followed him out of the cave into the inviting warmth of the day. She sat on the rock table by the oleander while George spread out a bandana and removed the lunch from the basket: a small bottle of retsina, which he handed to her, and bottles of water, followed by a loaf of bread, a square of feta wrapped in cheesecloth, a container of kalamata olives, and two plump tomatoes. He withdrew a serrated knife, napkins, plastic plates and glasses, and a piece of baklava.

"You've thought of everything," Claire said.

"With Alex's help," he said, smiling sheepishly. He pointed to the large triangle of pastry. "That's for you. Wait a minute, hold still. You have an insect in your hair. Let me." He positioned himself in front of her and removed a winged insect, holding it gently and then releasing it to the air. They were facing one another and very close. He placed a forefinger in the hollow of her collarbone and drew it lightly upwards, diagonally towards her ear, following its course with his eyes. Then he leaned in and settled his lips on hers, diffidently, asking permission.

Claire's eyes prickled with tears. She wanted to give him something back. "You know, I have thought of you ever since that night at the Ladases' when you pointed out the grease spot on my T-shirt."

"Works every time," George grinned.

"You know nothing about me."

"More than you think. I have my intuition—and other sources, even more reliable." He hunched his shoulders and brought his hands together. "Let's eat."

"What's Malta like?"

"Nothing to tell really. It's a rock."

"Of course I know that, but I've never been there. Say something in Maltese," Claire said, slicing a piece of bread.

George uttered a few words in his native language. "That was 'please pass the knife.'"

"Oh, sorry." She laughed and gave him the knife. "It sounds Italian."

"It is partly, part Sicilian and part Arabic." George put a tomato on his plate and sliced it with a deliberateness that reminded her of his kiss.

"Where did you learn English?"

"In school. It's actually the official language, or was."

The feta was delicious—moist, crumbly, sharp. Claire was feeling joy for the first time in months. Her senses vibrated with the presence of the strange man, his promising kiss, the salty cheese and piney wine on her tongue, the warmth of the sun on her skin, the air infused with the sweetness of the oleander. She felt more than simply reconnected to life; she was being swallowed up by it, immersed in a wonderful bright darkness that was like facing the sun with eyelids closed, a luminous half-sleep reminding her of the period before Sophie's birth. George's kiss had been another annunciation, and one that would have, within her lifetime, a middle and an end. Unlike Sophie's birth, it would assume in Claire's life the form of a story. She knew that because she wrote stories, and because she was forty-six.

They were in a network of sun and shadow. "Shall we move over there?" Claire asked, pointing to the sunnier bank of the riverbed. George got up immediately. Claire picked up the plate of baklava and they crossed over. Removing the cellophane from the pastry, she offered some to him.

"Never eat sweets," he said, opening a bottle of water and lying down against the slope of the bank.

"You said that all caves aren't—my silly word—'cosy'." Claire picked up the sticky dessert with her hands. George had forgotten forks, and the lapse was somehow reassuring.

"Quite the opposite," he laughed. "Dangerous, in fact. The one I'm in now, for instance, has to be climbed. It has steep pitches, precipices, and, in some places, we think, ice that never melts. Night and day don't exist. It amounts to mountain climbing in complete darkness, except for the light we provide, and in very cold temperatures. There were, though, several flat chambers and passageways before it got rough. It was in those first rooms they found some artifacts. There won't be any more of those where we're going now. At least I don't think so."

"Why keep going then?" Claire licked the honey-coated crumbs from her fingers.

"Well, what we find will be interesting to other scientists, geologists and biologists, as well as to amateur cave climbers. It has to be mapped."

"Why hasn't it been explored before? After all, it's been there for ever."

"Yes, but nobody knew it. It took an earthquake last year to uncover it. The quake was barely felt, didn't do any damage, but it was enough to reposition a boulder that had been hiding the entrance for centuries. The archaeologists have found objects dating back to Minoan times."

Claire had finished her dessert and was lying on the ground beside him, hoping for an embrace, but George looked at his watch and stood up. "Perhaps we should start back," he said, beginning to gather the remains of lunch.

They started down the riverbed towards the path when suddenly Claire, startled by a large bee buzzing close to her ear, stumbled and fell to the ground. As George helped her to her feet, she tried to make light of it, insisting it was nothing, but the heels of her palms, which had taken the brunt of the fall, stung, and she had scraped her knees on the rock. George noticed blood on one of them and, kneeling and dousing a napkin with the bottled water from the basket, gently dabbed at the wound. Then he produced a bandage from the small nylon pack around his waist and placed it on the spot. Claire used the rest of the water to wash away the dirt from her hands, and they started up again. As they passed a large aloe plant, several bees were moving in and out of its tall spike of chartreuse flowers. "It's taken that plant fifteen to twenty years to flower," George informed her, "and now it will die within a few weeks."

The path traversed a protected valley of olive and almond groves, with Italian cypresses here and there, marking a small church or dwelling. Claire had admired the scene from the main road but had never entered it. Eleni Pappadopoulos had been raised in Kalamos, in her grandfather's house. She had grown up looking down on the valley, walked through it to get to school, played among its trees and rocks with friends, and later, perhaps, met Aleko there to make love.

They finally came upon the main road, the rough uphill part now behind them. "How long are you staying in Kythera?" George asked as they walked quickly down the paved surface towards Kapsali. They were passing a roadside shrine, a white box on a post with offerings to the icon within a glass-framed door, objects ranging from half-empty packs of cigarettes and jars of honey to family photographs. Claire had been told that such locations along the road were chosen because accidents had occurred there. George repeated his question.

"I'm not sure," Claire replied. "What about you?"

"I'll be going to Crete soon. My work has to be finished before the rains begin. Tell me, do you miss your country?"

"Not really. My family, yes. Sophie, that's my daughter, and little Annabel—my granddaughter. But not my life there. It's too complicated. I think I would like to let go of it."

"Like the bait in the monkey trap."

"The what?"

"Have you ever seen a monkey trap? It's a hollowed gourd with bait inside it. The monkey reaches in and wraps his fist around the bait but can't remove his hand unless he drops the bait."

"And?"

"He never does." They walked a while in silence. "Have you ever been to Crete?"

"No."

"You should come. There's a small, very pleasant hotel, which used to be the British Consulate, on the outskirts of Chania. The Ladases' flat is on the top floor. It has a large terrace overlooking the sea and a small kitchen. I stay there when I'm not at the camp. If the Ladases are in Crete, I just rent another room in the hotel. It also has a dining room and bar. It's very quiet—and cosy, Clairaki." Claire recognized the affectionate Greek diminutive. George looked at her tenderly. "Like caves." They had reached the *Spitia* Vasili and were at the bottom of her bungalow steps.

"Will you come up?" Claire looked at George in such a way that he could not miss the subtext of her invitation.

"I have to call Crete. May I—come up—later? About seven?" Claire remembered she wanted to check in on Zoe and was glad of the delay.

"Perfect. Don't be late."

"Tell me about them, George."

"Well, Clairaki, the sounds you hear are produced by the males. They vibrate the drum-like membranes that are on their abdomens. It's a love call." They had been making love, soft, dark and wordless, their heartbeats throbbing with the sound of the cicadas. "They have only about a month more to live, like the aloe we saw today, so they're desperate to mate. They've been buried in the soil and living off plant juice for maybe as long as seven years."

"All that time in the dark!" Claire exclaimed, at the same time thinking that she wouldn't mind seven years in this cosy moonlit darkness, her body curved into his. Cicada love.

"Clairaki," he said, burying his face in her neck, "you must come to Crete."

10

GEORGE WAS CALLED TO CRETE and had been gone almost a week when Zoe and Claire drove into Potamos for the art and wine festival. "How are you feeling?" Claire asked, studying her friend behind the wheel. She hadn't spent time with Zoe since the afternoon of her confession and so welcomed this opportunity to talk.

"Fine," Zoe replied emphatically, defensively.

"You're—."

"Just fine," she said more softly. Zoe sighed, raked her fingers through her hair, and stared silently straight ahead at the road. She was an expert at the dramatic pause. "Sorry," she said finally, looking over to Claire. "It's the good thing about doctoring. You lose yourself really—in other people's problems, their bodies, their psyches."

"I'm glad you're better."

"Today, for example, I had a big surprise. Oh, by the way, I have a vacation in two weeks when a substitute comes over from Athens, and I've decided to join the Ladases in Crete. The timing is perfect. Why don't you come with me? A change of scene, and—George will be there." She smiled, and Claire wondered how Zoe knew about that development.

"Harry," Zoe said, reading her mind.

"Harry Smythe?"

"I haven't met him," Zoe replied, "but I gather he's not very good at secrets."

"Well, you'll meet him tonight. Tell me about the surprise you had at work today."

"I wish I could," Zoe said, "but, of course, I can't. Physician/patient confidentiality, you know."

"Leave out the names," Claire suggested.

"Yes, I guess I could do that. Well, today a woman came in with gynecological problems, some pain and irregular bleeding. I gave her a pelvic exam. Claire, she was a virgin!"

"There still are some you know."

"Oh yes," Zoe smiled, "I failed to mention she's married. She's in her mid-forties and has been married more than twenty-five years." Claire had a sudden insight. Eleni.

It was almost dark by the time they entered Potamos and found a parking place near the square. A number of people, European tourists mainly, were already there, strolling from booth to booth, sampling wines and buying commemorative mugs. Waiters were setting up tables in the roped-off street between their cafés and the square to augment their space for the expected overflow.

Claire and Zoe walked in the opposite direction, towards the church, then turned into a side street and entered a tall iron gate in need of a fresh coat of green paint. A broken concrete path led to the front steps of the old neoclassical house. Most of these on the island were derelict, the Greeks preferring the newer, more vernacular type, but a local merchant family had purchased this one, painted all the interior walls white, and imported track lighting from Athens for displaying art. The exterior stucco walls were faded and pocked, the garden overgrown. The front door was open.

They passed the first room—exclusively banal landscapes and trite renditions of tourist attractions—and entered another one, more promising, where Harry Smythe was speaking German to a tourist couple. The plexiglass-encased card on the wall read "States of Consciousness" and gave the artist's name. Claire looked up to see Harry introducing himself to Zoe, who had already begun circling the room. He must have seen Zoe come in with her. She watched the two assess one another as they conversed and remembered having considered them a possible twosome.

Claire was drawn immediately to one of the oils, predominantly dark gray with cloudy spirals of lighter gray and flecks of green, black, yellow and white towards the edges. She felt an instant familiarity with it. The painting brought to mind the time of her pregnancy, her animal vagueness and sense of living in a place such as that. For nine months she had been almost as unconscious as the foetus within her, like a fish finning its way through murky shallows, where now and then filaments of light penetrate the surface and illuminate the entangled weeds of a vegetable world. She had felt disconnected for those nine months, at least from things she normally found important, and now she began to see that strange disengagement in another light. It had been, in fact, a primary connectedness—to nature she supposed. But what did that mean exactly? Zoe and Harry had joined her.

"I've heard there's food and drink," Harry said. "Shall we go look for it?" The women accompanied him down the hall and around a corner into a huge old-fashioned kitchen, where a group of people were helping themselves to *meze* laid out on a worktable, along with carafes of white wine and bottles of water. There were several non-Greek tourists and a few Greeks, some of the artists perhaps, among them.

"Where are the Ladases' paintings?" Claire asked Harry, who was handing her a glass of wine.

"Upstairs. My friend's work is there as well, across the hall. But why don't we have a rest first? Let's sit out here on the back porch and have our wine."

They stepped out into the warm night, fragrant with honeysuckle. The vine had wound itself around the wrought iron railing and was making its way up the side of the house to the second floor. Zoe and Harry began to exchange the tentative questions and answers of people just introduced. There was no moon, and the only light was that coming from the kitchen window. Claire plucked one of the creamy, trumpet-shaped blooms from the honeysuckle, feeling its softness between her fingers, and watched people behind the window, a bright yellow rectangle against the dark wall, a canvas of sorts. But the reality—half a face, then a disembodied arm, then two faces in profile—seemed less arbitrary, more like art, than the so-called realistic paintings in the first room. A head, which looked as if it might belong to Eleni Pappadopolous, passed by.

Claire tossed the flower to the ground and took a sip of wine. "You know those 'consciousness' paintings we just saw—they remind me of an article I read recently about sleep and wakefulness. They found that people who slept more soundly were more fully awake in their non-sleep period."

"That's obvious," Zoe said. "Look at old people not sleeping well at night and nodding off during the day."

"Yes, I know," Claire replied. "But what interests me is just that. The oppositions of sleep and wakefulness come together, sort of blur, as we approach death. The study was actually trying to answer the question of why we sleep, why it's necessary, not just for good health but for life itself. If rats are kept awake for a long period of time, they simply die. And the only conclusion they could draw was that this is just the way it is, just the way biological systems operate. They could find no other reason—if you can call that a reason."

"Hmm. Interesting. Sort of a dialectic of existence," Harry said. "Tell me, have you heard from George?"

"Just once. He called when he arrived in Chania, before leaving for the mountains." Claire had continued to feel his presence, as though she had somehow internalized him. She looked forward to seeing George again without feeling, in the meantime, anxious and impatient. His absence, unlike that of past lovers, had not translated to an aching void. "Anyway, I'll be seeing him in a couple of weeks. I'm going to Crete with Zoe. We're staying at the hotel where the Ladases have an apartment."

"So am I," Harry announced. "Actually, I've never been to the 'fair and fertile Crete.' I really must see it."

"That's wonderful." Claire said. He definitely added something.

"Great," Zoe put in, apparently feeling the same. She rose. "Well, I think I'm ready for more art."

When they reached the top of the stairs, Zoe swung around the door jamb of the Ladases' room and waved jauntily at Alex. Claire noticed the German couple she had seen Harry with downstairs examining a painting and conferring in low tones. Zeno, his back to the door, was standing apart from it all, looking out of a pair of tall windows that were open and letting in the sweet, silky air. Claire knew he hated these things, was shy about presenting his work to the public. Harry led Zoe and Claire into the room opposite, where the works of several artists were displayed.

He pointed out the paintings he had brought from London, and Claire, having assumed his friend Chris was a man, now realized she had been wrong. All three paintings were of women with their children, and they conveyed not so much how maternity looked as how it felt. A man simply could not have done them. She read the artist's name, Christine Cox. A romantic friendship? The best of the three paintings was of a nursing mother with large breasts, a placid face and an incomplete head. The bit of missing skull reminded Claire of Alex's unfinished "Daphne." That would be finished now, she realized, and suddenly was anxious to see it. After a cursory look at the other works, she left Zoe and Harry to go across the hall.

The "Daphne" *was* finished. The area of thin pencil strokes on naked canvas had been brought forward with warm flesh tones and rich greens. It was the focal center of the room, and a crowd had gathered around it, captivated by the agonized twisting of the human body into a tree-trunk, by woman becoming laurel. Where else but in the metamorphoses of Greek mythology reside such mysterious movement and fluidity, such sinuous images of becoming? "It's wonderful, Alex," Claire said. She was still standing in front of it when Zoe and Harry came up behind her.

"Lovely," Harry said.

"A feminine victory," Zoe added. "By becoming a tree, she has escaped her pursuer for ever."

"Yes," Harry said, "but for centuries her leaves will crown the heads of victorious male athletes." Zoe closed her eyes in mock disdain. "By the way, Zeno said we should get down to the square and claim a table soon. He and Alex can't get away until ten when the gallery closes."

Claire turned from the painting and saw Eleni and her mother, Tula, enter the room. It had been Eleni in the kitchen window. She was wearing her hair in a new way, divided into two braids, brought up and fastened at the top of her head. Claire guessed that Eleni was aware of the painting for which she had sat and must have been curious about the finished canvas. "What do you think, Eleni?" Claire asked. They were standing side by side, gazing at the transformation of Daphne. "I think her face is yours."

"Yes," Eleni replied, blushing. Claire looked from the real woman to the painted one, noting the resemblances. Eleni seemed transfixed. "Today I make a syrup cake for you," she said, without taking her eyes from the painting. "I give it to *Kyria* Vasili to put in your kitchen. Another recipe."

"Thank you, Eleni. That's very kind. I'll look forward to it." Claire observed the woman beside her in the context of Zoe's new information. Of course, the married virgin might not be Eleni at all, but somehow she felt it had to be. She thought of how she had envied Eleni and wished that her own life had been as simple and unchanging. But by staying in the same loveless marriage, fixed to her birthplace, she had probably suffered more than Claire. In her somatic stillness, Eleni had felt more strongly, perhaps, the sweeping currents of life. Her psyche might well be as twisted and tortured as the torso of the wood nymph. How could anyone bear the turbulence of existence without the loosening of sex and the leavening of love? Claire looked at her watch and saw it was almost nine-thirty. She glanced around the room and, not seeing Zoe or Harry, excused herself to go and find them. As she reached the door, she turned around for one last look at the "Daphne." Eleni was still looking at the painting.

11

CLAIRE, SNUG WITH ZOE AND their smaller bags in the back seat of the taxi, turned to look down at Kapsali as Yiannis drove towards the glarey stucco streak of the Chora. The bay below looked puckery—a seersucker sea, its flat smooth surface of the past few weeks ruffled as wind moved over the water.

"Is this the 'cucumber wind' from Arabia?" Claire asked Zoe. Eleni had told her about it. The Greeks called it that because they believed its warmth ripened the cucumbers.

"No, Claire. The cucumbers are ripe already, haven't you noticed? This is our typical summer northwesterly, the *meltemi*."

It was the fifteenth of August, the biggest festival of summer, and the women were on their way to Crete. The Ladases were already in Chania, and Harry intended to take the night-ferry over. Zoe had thought it would be a good day for them to fly, for most people were already where they wanted to be for the celebration. They would stay in Athens that night. Zoe wanted to see her parents, and Claire looked forward to having some time in the city where she had spent almost two years of her life.

Zoe had been right about travelling on that day. When they entered the small one-room terminal, there were just a few people standing in line to have themselves and their baggage weighed. Claire joined the queue, Zoe falling in behind her. The weighing-in procedure before boarding small planes always unnerved her, the implication that a few pounds could make the difference between a safe flight and a risky one, or that the distribution of weight should matter at all. She remembered the pilot on her incoming flight to the island moving passengers from side to side and front to back for balance, as though a heavy person or several of them could actually tip the plane.

"Eleni!" Zoe exclaimed. Claire turned around to see the Greek woman and her mother enter the building. The plane was coming from Athens and depositing passengers before flying back, so she assumed they were expecting friends or relatives from the mainland. But then she saw a taxi driver come into the terminal and place a suitcase by their side. Perhaps Tula was leaving.

"I go to Athens," Eleni announced, smiling her toothy smile and moving into line. "My first time." She embraced Tula, who declared she had to get to church, and watched as her mother left the terminal and climbed back into the cab. "I'm happy you go too. I don't like airplanes."

"Flying is very safe," Claire said, beginning to lose her own trepidations in reassuring the woman. Something extraordinary must have decided Eleni to leave her island, Claire thought—a funeral, perhaps, or a crucial medical examination.

"I think it's wonderful you're making this trip," Zoe said. "Are you visiting someone?"

"I go to meet my cousin Serena," Eleni said. "She comes from Australia, and I haven't seen her since we were girls. She likes Athens. She writes a letter to meet her there, but I don't want to. So I write that she comes to Kythera to see me." Eleni's eyes were bright with excitement.

"But you changed your mind," Zoe said.

"Yes. Alex's painting, I think."

"The 'Daphne.'"

"Yes." Eleni paused. "I saw something. I try to explain. When I was a girl I dream of ships with purple sails, and then of Italian fishing boats with handsome fishermen. Then—."

"And then—?" Claire was astonished. Eleni had told her about Serena, but not about her girlhood daydreams. She had somehow intuited them. Of course, the Eleni of her novel had actually met a handsome young fisherman, but it was probable that Eleni's dreams had been generated by a similar experience.

"Then—I stop dreaming." Suddenly overcome with shyness, Eleni blushed and looked down at her hands. There was a shattering sound. The plane from Athens had landed and was roaring down the runway.

A busload or two of Japanese tourists were all over the lobby, at the front desk, in the gift shop, three-deep in front of the elevators. Zoe and Claire elected to use the stairs. "Tourists!" Claire said vehemently as they began their climb.

"George hasn't reformed you, I see."

"What do you mean?" The stairwell was cool, the tomb-like marble a relief after the hot, sticky cab ride from the airport.

"Haven't you noticed that George dislikes tourists berating other tourists? 'We're all tourists here,' I heard him say once, and he didn't mean Greece."

Claire fell behind Zoe and thought of George's silence that day down at the cove when she had been fulminating against cruise ships. She blushed at the recollection. Her tirade probably had offended him. "Part of his charm, don't you think?" Zoe continued, turning to check her friend's progress. "He doesn't make the distinctions the rest of us do. He's too good." She slowed down as they approached the third floor, and Claire had a chance to catch up with her. When they arrived at the fourth floor, they saw their porter, an elderly man, step off the service elevator. They followed him as he struggled with their luggage down the long dark hall and waited while he fumbled with the key, opened the door, and deposited the bags inside. Claire took the key and gave him many more drachmas than custom required.

The room was frigid. Zoe kicked off her shoes and, with a long sigh, fell back on one of the beds. Claire turned off the air-conditioning, opened the double window, and, leaning against the sill, looked down into the green well of a courtyard. There was a rectangle of grass, a boxwood hedge, and sculpted globes of shrubbery in large pots. The liquid warble of pigeons could be heard above the noise of Athens, which was muted at that height, a humming presence that was pleasant and unintrusive. She collapsed on an armchair by the window. A panel of sheer white curtain blew in on a breeze and landed, smelling of dusty nylon, on her shoulder.

"Back to George—"

"George?" Zoe smiled, teasing.

"Yes. You mentioned him, remember? His goodness. He is very good, isn't he? Exquisitely kind. But you're probably more objective than I am, and you've known him a little longer. Can you fault him at all? I mean about anything?" Claire took a nectarine from the complimentary fruit on a table beside her chair and passed the bowl to Zoe. They were having dinner that night with Zoe's parents and had decided to skip lunch.

"No, Claire, I agree with you. Well, I guess if I had to find a fault—." Zoe took a banana, studied it, and put it back in the bowl. She looked at her watch.

"Yes?"

"I think he's a little careless sometimes."

"Careless?"

"Yes. You know, about his health—his safety." She was abstracted. Her mind had moved on to something else.

"Hmm, I know what you mean. Those awful caves." Zoe was off the bed, putting on her shoes, and Claire remembered then that she was going to church. She considered accompanying her, thinking it might be interesting. "Tell me about today's festival. What exactly is it?" Zoe took a lipstick and hairbrush from her purse and went into the bathroom.

"It's the holiday of the Kimesis, or Sleeping of the Virgin. The Feast of the Assumption to Westerners." She was shouting her explanation from the bathroom. "Some places here actually have funeral ceremonies and processions, like Christ's at Easter." She came to the door, hairbrush in hand. "I think the meaning of the feast is in the icons. They show Mary dead on the bier and Christ behind her with her soul, in the form of an infant, in his arms. Quite a reversal, isn't it?"

"How so?"

"Well," Zoe began, waving the hairbrush for emphasis. "Now Christ is the mother. It is he who has given life, and the human mother has been outdone because the life that Christ gives is immortal. You see, the death of Mary is actually the death of female divinity. Clever, isn't it? Goodbye, Gaia. *Adio* Athena, Artemis, Aphrodite!" She turned on her heel and was back in the bathroom. Claire thought of the icon at the monastery in Kythera, the madonna with the blacked-out face. Empty like the eyes of the Buddha, she had thought when she saw it that day, characterless, featureless, and therefore divine. Now, after Zoe's comments, she saw it in another light, as perhaps less, not more, than human—an obliteration, a mere vessel for birth and nurture. Not unlike the painting they had seen at Potamos of the nursing mother with the incomplete head. Not unlike her somnolent self in the nine months before Sophie.

"It's the separation of body and soul," Zoe said.

"Yes, that's where we went wrong," Claire said, understanding then the feminists' call for a female God. It was, after all, a way back to wholeness.

At seven o'clock, the women were in a taxi, creeping through the old neighborhood of Psyrri. Claire had asked the driver to take them there before getting on the busy boulevard to Glyfada, where Zoe's parents lived. She and John had explored the area on weekends in conjunction with browsing the flea market. What she now saw from the taxi window was an assault to her memory of "old Athens." The shock of change felt physical, a blow to the brain, where experience had made a specific imprint of what had been. That came before the nostalgia and sense of loss. The dark, snaky streets, once quaint and intact, were obstacle courses of broken-up macadam and roped-off sections protecting pedestrians from pits and trenches. Zoe explained that the pavements were being widened. New buildings rose beyond the scope of the eye. In the narrowness of the street, it was impossible to see the tops of them. There was a bright, shiny arcade of stores where once had been a dusty old gramophone shop, a whimsical cornucopia of amplifying horns. But Claire did recognize a café, and locals still sat talking at tables on the sidestreets with their wine, cigarettes and *meze*.

Zoe's childhood home was an anomaly for Athens, an old half-timbered mock Tudor, dwarfed by and in the shadow of a blocky new two-storey duplex just a few yards from the front door. Hari and Thespina embraced their daughter and her friend and stepped aside as they entered the sitting room. Zoe followed her mother through a narrow arch into the kitchen, and Claire, at Hari's invitation, sank into a sofa, which was striped with warm pinkish bands of sunlight coming through the venetian blinds behind it. Hari, still rumpled from his afternoon nap, was talkative and flirtatious and asked her a series of questions about California. His daughter, having lived there, would have told him everything he wanted to know, but it was a conversational bridge and an opportunity to use his limited English, which he appeared to revel in. Zoe and her mother brought out plates of *meze* from the kitchen and set them on a small tea table. Thespina's English was more hesitant but better than Hari's, and she perched on the arm of the sofa to show Claire baby pictures of Zoe.

An hour later they left for the restaurant, where that evening, Thespina had mentioned, there would be Cretan music and dance. They walked to the corner and turned into the street that ran diagonally from the city into the boulevard along the waterfront. This suburb was next to the one where Claire and John had lived, and, again, she felt the jolting disorientation of change. The street, then narrow and unpaved, had become a busy four-lane thoroughfare. But the inhabitants were still walking it as they had done then, enjoying the warm night air, the smell of seafood and potatoes frying in oil, apparently oblivious to the pollution and traffic. And they were still sitting out on their balconies, eating, drinking and talking with friends. Later, they would drag mattresses from stuffy bedrooms out to these same balconies to sleep in the cooler open air. At that time of year all Athens moved outside, and there was an atmosphere of celebration as if summer itself were but one long festival. Zoe had said the restaurant was a steak house, and within a block of it they began to smell the tantalizing aroma of grilled meat and oregano.

They had finished their steaks when Claire noticed that the crowd had thinned. Those remaining appeared to be tourists, and she was discomfited by the thought that Zoe and her parents probably would not have stayed had it not been for their foreign guest. The waiters were scurrying about, removing dishes and pulling away tables to make a clearing for the folkloric. A lively folk dance, accompanied by the bouzouki, bagpipes and lyre, was followed by another and then another. Zoe named them for Claire, a *sousta*, a *syrtos*, a *kastrinos*. The costume and choreography of each dance was traditional to Crete. But "choreography" wasn't really the right word. It was like using the word "art" for icons. These dances, like the icons, were more an expression of tradition than an innovation.

Claire was feeling sleepy and wishing it would end. Finally there came a lull. Perhaps it was over. The dancers seemed to be leaving, and then the musicians. But the lyre-player remained, an imperious-looking, hollow-eyed man dressed in black, sitting on a stool in the center of the makeshift stage. Several moustached men in baggy breeches, boots and waistcoats filed into the clearing and made a circle around him. The musician was bent over his instrument, trying the strings, and then he began to play, slowly at first. There was a feeling of anticipation as the pace gradually increased. Claire closed her eyes and saw the contours of the music, the balletic arcs, lines and swirls, all carved out of silence. Perhaps that was the purpose of life, to give shape to things through art. Or, if not that, at least to lead a shapely life—the thing she had failed to do, that she had imagined Eleni was doing, that poor Sophie was striving for. Perhaps that was, after all, the only point to creation. Form might be enough. Why should we look further? God was neither a moralist nor a theologian, certainly not a humanitarian. He was an artist.

The music had reached its peak, its rhythm become frenzied and driven. Claire opened her eyes. The dancers were bobbing rapidly, heads and torsos scarcely moving, their arms held stiffly at their sides as their legs obeyed the beat of the music. They were like puppets to the lyre-player's puppeteer. And then, without warning, the musician broke off, and the dance was over. Claire was puzzled by the suddenness of it, and Zoe said that was how the *pentozalis* always ended. Hari laughed and said the dance was like life.

THE LYRE-PLAYER

12

THE PLANE WAS MAKING SICKENING leaps around the sky. Claire said to herself that she could not be dying now, that such an end was not appropriate given all that had gone before, not equal to the sum of her life's events. For she believed her life, shapeless as it was, did have some inner logic, that it unfolded itself from within. In that way it was like a story. But, of course, the Great Lyre-Player could take the aircraft out of the sky at any time he chose, without heed to individual equations or artful finales, and the bereaved would nevertheless make up stories of consolation to give meaning to the event. "Better this than two more months of cancer"—"he died with his boots on"—"she died doing what she loved." Even the indifferent Lyre-Player was a story, one that painted in broad strokes something too large, or too subtle and minute, for our understanding. Magical thinking—coherence was always preferable to truth.

"This thing is old." Zoe looked over to Claire, raised her eyebrows, and gave her seat belt an extra tug. Claire, too, had noticed that the plane was older than any she had been on, the seats rigid and unadjustable, the windows tiny and oddly placed, the walls of rattling formica less rounded. She wiped her wet palms on her jeans and suddenly felt ill. She opened the seat pocket in front of her and gasped, "No sick bags?" Zoe looked alarmed and handed her an empty plastic bag from her purse. "Damn!" the doctor said as the plane made another diagonal jump. Claire's stomach had settled down for the moment, and the emergency of being sick gave way again to fear. She looked around at their fellow passengers. Many were crossing themselves or fingering worry-beads. A baby was screaming. "We won't go down. Too many children," Zoe said, also looking around. She believed in an ultimate justice, Claire thought, despite overwhelming evidence to the contrary.

They landed safely, their benighted superstitions not only intact but further entrenched. They had not gone down. For many passengers, a merciful God had heard their appeals. For Zoe, justice had prevailed. And, for Claire, life was still story. She pulled her suitcase off the carousel and followed Zoe out of the terminal. It was as windy as it had been in Kythera the day before. Alex was in her car at the curb, waving and tooting the horn to get their attention. They piled their luggage in the trunk of the small Renault and got in. It was a relic, the paint finish gone, leaving only a suggestion of the original blue, and the interior torn, exposing in places the frame and the springs and stuffing of the seats. Alex tried the ignition a couple of times, and the car lurched forward.

"Zeno's down at the harbor, Harry is probably asleep—arrived early this morning, and George will be coming down off the mountain this afternoon." Alex sent Claire a conspiratorial glance and patted her hand. As they drove south down the broad peninsula towards Chania, Claire noticed how different the topography was from that of Kythera, how the mountain range in the distance rose so abruptly from the flatness of the plain. She gazed at the mountains and thought of George there, *in* them really, doing his strange exploration.

"Is he over there?" she asked Alex, pointing to the range.

"No, farther east. You're looking at the Madra Vouna, or White Mountains. He's on the central Ida massif." Claire found the landscape slightly unsettling, for it might have been any number of other places. When they entered the outskirts of Chania, she was pleased by the more identifiable urban scene, the serried white dwellings, signs and billboards in Cyrillic lettering, glittering sea and pebbly shore. It could be nowhere, after all, but Greece.

"Our hotel, The Daedalus, is on this side of Chania in the district of Halepa," Alex said, "so we won't see the town now. It's walking distance though, takes about fifteen minutes to walk from the hotel to the center, and there you have both old and new next to each other and the wonderful harbor. You might try doing that after lunch." Claire knew that she would sleep after lunch. They had been up late the night before, and the few hours' sleep combined with the morning's rough flight had taken its toll.

Alex turned left into a gated gravel driveway, drove past the front of the old consulate, a shabby white neoclassical structure, and parked in a space to the left of it. Luggage in hand, they crossed the gravel and climbed the tiled steps to the entrance. A marble relief of the winged Daedalus was above the door.

The lobby was a small sitting room, and the noon sun streaming through ruddy curtains gave it a pleasant amber glow. There was a fireplace, a mixture of Greek and English furnishings, and old photographs of well-dressed English people covering the walls. Alex, on her way up the stairs, suggested that Claire and Zoe meet her for lunch in the dining room after they had settled. Claire handed her charge card to the woman behind the desk and left Zoe to ask questions and get the keys. She sat down on a Greek divan of carved dark wood and admired its heavy yellow skirt of embroidered flowers and birds and the delicate lace-trimmed white cotton on the seat and back cushions. A woman appeared from behind a door next to the staircase with a tray of *koulourakia*, two tiny glasses of raki and large tumblers of water. She placed it on a sea-captain's trunk in front of the divan. Zoe handed Claire her room key and excused herself to go to the car for something she had left behind. Claire gnawed at an almond-flavored cookie and took a sip of the raki, which burned on its way down.

"Let's go up," Zoe said when she returned. Claire pointed to the tray. "Not hungry, thanks. By the way, there's no lift, so we'll get some exercise. My room's right across from yours. George didn't want to presume, of course, so you have a room to yourself." There was no one around for the luggage, so they climbed the stairs, clumsily dragging their bags behind them. When they reached the second floor, they heard loud laughter from the floor above. "Harry's up," Zoe said, smiling. Claire, too, recognized the infectious laugh.

Her room was small, clean and simply furnished. A lithograph of what she presumed to be Chania's harbor was at the head of the bed. A scratched-up mahoghany wardrobe, with a door that wouldn't close, covered most of one wall, and in a corner stood a table with a vase of carnations. Their sweetness mingled with the faint chlorine odor from the bathroom. The window overlooked the walled garden below, a haphazard profusion of flowers, tall dry weeds and empty pots, as well as a few authentic-looking architectural fragments. A rusty metal table and chair sat under a pepper tree. Claire was grateful for the room. Zoe's room, across the hall and down one, was on the front and exposed to the noisy street, although at the second floor level she might see a strip of sea over the tall front hedge. George's room was farther down, at the end of the hall.

George. Claire couldn't quite believe she would be seeing him in a matter of hours, be with him in that very room. It seemed a long time since she had seen him although it had been less than two weeks. Her memory of his face had even faded somewhat, but the feeling of warmth, wholeness and sexual quickening, the rock becoming molten, had stayed with her. He had healed her.

She was glad for the separate rooms as she began to unpack. There wasn't enough space for the belongings of two people, especially since she had packed a lot of clothing, not knowing how long she would be staying. Her landlady had kindly excused her from any rent during her absence and even provided her with storage space for those things she wanted to leave behind. She was enjoying this gradual shedding of possessions as she moved from large house, to bungalow, to hotel room. Pleased with this new abode, small and manageable, she climbed the red-and-black runnered stairs to the dining room on the third floor.

"Ah, here's Claire!" Harry exclaimed, rising from a table by a long stretch of window, which overlooked the boulevard and sea beyond. He, Alex, and Zoe were sitting next to one another, drinking white wine and poring over a stack of photographs Alex had taken the previous summer in Kythera. Claire sat down on the other side of the table where, presumably, Zeno would also be sitting. There were two place settings, minus the wine glasses, and Harry went up to the small bar, which separated the dining room from the kitchen beyond, to ask for another glass.

"That's wonderful of Chris," Alex commented, admiring one of the photographs and passing it to Harry. Claire thought it had to be the painter, Harry's English friend.

"An excellent likeness," Harry said, looking tenderly at the image. He passed it to Claire, and she saw that Chris was a much older woman than she had presumed. She had visualized a girlfriend, but Chris was a woman in her sixties with a strong Mediterranean face and very short gray hair.

"Ha, this is wonderful." Harry was looking at another one. "I must have a copy of this." He handed it to Alex and Zoe, who laughed and passed it to Claire. She examined the photograph of Zeno gutting a fish just as the man himself was coming through the door.

The dining room had once served as a library, and there were still a few hundred books on shelves lining the wood-panelled walls. Lunch had not yet come, so Claire circled the room, taking out some that interested her. There were quite a number of English classics, faded and worn by years of use and exposure to the damp air, and Greek books as well, some translated into English. One intriguing-looking volume, entitled *Oneirokrites* or "Dream Book," brought to Claire's mind the dream she had had the night before and forgotten about until just then. Maybe she could find it in the dream book.

The meal was being brought to the table, so Claire placed her book selections on the empty table behind them and sat down. She was very tired and, wanting a nap before George arrived, asked Zeno when he thought he would be coming.

"Probably late afternoon or evening. The cave is an hour and a half from Anogeia, and it takes about two and a half hours to get down here from that village. Here's a map." He reached into a pocket, pulled out a simplified tourist map of the island, and spread it out before her. With a green-paint-stained finger he pointed to the dot labelled Anogeia, and then drew an imaginary arc moving north and then west, along the littoral, to Chania. "George doesn't have a car, so he gets a ride to the village in one of the project's jeeps and then tries to find a young villager to drive him down. Or if that doesn't work, there's a bus route between Anogeia and Chania. If he comes on the bus, it will be later."

"We won't have dinner before he arrives," Alex said. The Ladases were cooking the evening meal, for which Zeno had been in town buying food. Claire withdrew from the conversation for a while to study the map. She saw the skull-shaped peninsula where they had landed that morning, at the neck of which Chania lay. She noted the two bays on either side of Chania, Suda Bay and Kastelli Kissamou, and broken red lines indicating ferry passages to Piraeus and other ports, including Kapsali. She could return to Kythera by boat if she chose. Harry had left the table to get another decanter of wine and, on his way back, he examined her book stack.

"Good choices," he said, sitting down again. He looked rather wistful and serious. She had taken Forster's *A Passage to India*, the collected poems of both Philip Larkin and Yeats, the tattered *Oneirokrites*, and *Tale of a Town*, by a man named Prevelakis.

Claire turned to Alex. "Do you know anything about *Oneirokrites*?"

"Oh, that's very important. Almost every family has a dream book, just as they have a Bible. It describes common dreams and gives interpretations, which are sometimes prophetic. There're many such books, and they change all the time."

Alex turned around and extracted the book from the pile. She opened the cover and checked the date. "This is an old one, 1938. They have to bring them up to date because our dreams change with the times."

"Hmm, I always thought they were timeless," Claire remarked. "If you have a flying dream, your sex life is good, falling is something else— can't remember, a death means a wedding, a wedding means a death."

"Maybe some dreams are—universal that is," Zeno said, "but most are cultural."

"But look at Freud," Zoe said. "His dream analysis was based on human psychology, and that's universal."

"Yes," Zeno replied, "but the images and interpretations are cultural— have to be. I'll give you an example. Artemidoros, a professional dream interpreter in the second century, wrote the first dream book. People then spent a lot of time in religious observation, tending to statues and icons, anointing them, cleaning them, sweeping in front of them, and their dreams of those objects reflected that closeness. Modern Greeks also dream of statues and icons, but there is less intimacy with those objects now, so the interpretations are different. And, as you might guess, they're less prophetic and more psychological."

"And Americans and Englishmen don't dream of those at all," Harry said, getting up from the table, leaving most of the food on his plate. "Excuse me, but I've got to get some sleep. See you tonight."

"Around eight," Alex said.

"Americans and Englishmen don't dream of those at all." Claire was thinking of Harry's remark. She had dreamt of the icon at Myrtidion, but evidently there was no point in looking it up in a 1938 dream book. The idea that the dream during that time would have meant something different from what it meant now intrigued her. Of course it was all nonsense, another frail attempt at coherence. Claire undressed, drew back the bedcovers and took up the Prevelakis book. A pleasant afternoon hum came through the window, a muffled traffic drone mixed with some bird and insect sounds from the garden below. Looking down, she saw a cat on the solitary chair under the pepper tree. It was on its haunches, alert, and ready to pounce on something. She lay down on her side and, propping her head on her hand, opened the book.

The pages she flipped through had a musty smell, faintly nostalgic, comforting. Something caught her eye. *The Christian painter is little different from the monk, even if he does live in towns and even if he does have dealings with the world. As the monk kneels to pray to God, so the icon-painter sits down on his stool and picks up his brushes to paint. His work is a prayer too, although rather than murmuring the words he paints them. Thus he must be pure in heart, his tongue must be free of vulgar words and his hands must be clean. Before touching his brushes and his paints, he must prepare: he must fast, he must read the brief life of the saint whose story he will be illustrating, and he must enter into the life and martyrdom of that saint. His soul must be clear as crystal, and only then will Divine Grace descend on him and the holy icon will flow from his brush. Here, the painter does not boast of his work, and he must not insert into it anything from his own things or the cares of his life, as other painters do. Here the icon is the gift of God, and the painter is the conduit of his spirit.* Claire lifted her eyes from the page, *...he must not insert into it anything from his own things.* She liked that. Her eyelids were heavy. She put down the book and dropped into a deep slumber.

There was a tap on the door. For a moment, Claire was disoriented, thinking she was back in Kythera. Then she remembered and realized the person in the hall had to be Zoe, or maybe even George. With a rush of excitement, she leapt out of bed, called out to wait a minute, and checked her appearance in the bathroom mirror. She ran a damp cloth over her face and drew up her hair. She opened the door and there was George, weary and smiling. A narrow shaft of sunlight sliding in through a small window at the end of the otherwise dark hall created a soft bright edge around his head. How, she wondered, moved to tears, could she ever have thought him anything but handsome.

Without a word, he stepped into the room and drew her to him, kissing her lightly around the mouth, barely touching her lips, teasing her in that way so that she ached for him. They didn't walk to the bed but were suddenly there. They didn't undress but were naked. Afterwards, they slept for an hour or more. When Claire awoke, George was still asleep, and she went quietly into the bathroom to shower. When she returned to the bedroom, he was up and dressed.

He peered down into the garden, ran his hand over the rosy bedcover, and looked around the room. "Cosy," he said, looking very happy. "I'll get us some tea." He opened the door, and the hall was dark again.

The Ladases' apartment was on the third floor next to the dining room and across from Harry's room. It was a simple and small space, except for the spectacular terrace, long and wide, from which could be seen a broad expanse of the Cretan sea and, to the left, the remainder of the road they had taken from the airport, ending in a copse of trees, the only splash of green in the composition. George pointed to where, near the trees, the limestone wall of the old Venetian harbor began. Alex was setting the table on the terrace, and Zoe and Zeno were sitting on one of the couches inside, smoking and arguing about something. Harry hadn't yet come across the hall.

"Why can't the sky just stay like that?" Claire asked George. The western sky was a deep pink—cyclamen pink she had decided, having read that the flower was indigenous to Crete. "And this moment—being here with you, the view, those smells coming from the kitchen, these wonderful friends. Tell me, George." He smiled. "Mainly being here with you. Anywhere with you, I think." He picked her hand up off the ledge and kissed it, a sweet and solemn gesture.

Claire had been trying to imagine a future with George, for she knew she would never leave him and believed his love for her to be a permanent thing. In her habit of looking at life as story, Claire saw a break-up as impossible but, strangely, could not conceive of a future together either. The idea of George in California, grandfathering Annabel, seemed absurd. She in Malta, equally absurd—she couldn't even imagine the place. Would she follow him up mountains and learn how to weave? Nothing made sense, except that she was perfectly happy in his company.

"That love you have for the present, the fullness of it—and the sensuality of it—it has a dark side you know," George said, lifting a strand of hair off her face and placing his hand on her cheek, already warm with the wine. There was an outburst of laughter from inside, and they knew that Harry had arrived. Zoe brought a pitcher of red wine, bread, and olives to the table, and they all sat down.

"Did you get some sleep?" George asked Harry.

"Yes," he smiled, "and I dreamt of statues."

"No!" Zoe exclaimed.

"Hmm." Zeno looked serious. "Were you a statue yourself, or did you just see one?"

Harry laughed. "And what if I were the statue?" He poured more wine into his glass.

"That would not bode well. It would mean that something had gone wrong in your emotional life."

"And if I simply saw one?"

"Then you've met your ideal."

"'Live lips upon a plummet-measured face,'" Harry said, raising his glass to Zoe. Alex brought a large hot casserole to the table, and then what she called an "American-style" salad of lettuce and tomatoes.

"Let's all go to the beach tomorrow," Zoe proposed, helping herself to the steaming food.

"I want to see the town," Claire said. "George and I are walking there in the morning."

"I'm afraid Zeno and I can't join you," Alex said. "It's a busy day at the gallery." She turned to George. "Don't forget to bring Claire by in the morning."

"Why don't you and Claire meet Zoe and me in Rethymno in the afternoon?" Harry suggested. Claire had seen Rethymno on Zeno's map, just east of Chania. "We could have lunch there. Fish and chips, hamburgers, whatever you like. The place is swarming with tourists and their own native brands of fast food, but it's a beautiful beach— goes on for ever."

"You and Zoe can take our car," Zeno offered.

"Ha, the rotting Renault. I appreciate that, actually. But what about you two?" he said, turning to George and Claire.

"We'll get a taxi out to the beach," George said.

"Of course not," Harry said. "We'll all go together in the car. Zoe and I can wait till you get back from town."

"That suits me," Zoe said. "There're some things I want to do in the morning anyway." She points to her plate. "This is delicious."

Claire turned to Alex. "What is it?"

"Zeno put it together this afternoon with what he found at the market. A *briami* we call it, vegetables cooked together in the oven."

"A Greek man who can cook." Zoe looked at Zeno with admiration. "Why didn't I find you first?"

"Because I found him before you were born," Alex said. The faint sound of recorded music floated through the windows of the dining room next door. Claire recognized the opening of the theme music from *Zorba*. "There must be diners in the restaurant. They always feel they have to do that."

"I haven't seen anyone else around," Zoe said.

"There's only one other hotel guest at the moment, a photographer, but the dining room is a restaurant open to anyone. And it has a good reputation. In fact, guests have to make reservations if they want to eat there in the evening. How long will you be down this time?" Alex asked George.

"They want me back Wednesday."

Claire counted. They had four days. She hadn't considered the next separation. The music from the dining room had become louder, and Harry, who had been talking to Zoe, suddenly leapt from the table and began to dance, dragging Zeno along with him. Arm in arm, they mimicked the fancy footwork of the folk dance, Zeno doing a more credible job than the Englishman of course, both exaggerating the movements and mocking themselves. Zeno, lips compressed, looked serious, and Harry, holding back laughter, beamed like the Cheshire cat. They were a wonderful pair. Claire sat close to George, enjoying their antics and the heavy dark warmth of the starless night. The *meltemi* they had first felt in Kythera had finally subsided, bringing on a resurgence of insect life, the fluttering of moths in suicidal droves to the dim globe light above the door and the insistent whine of a mosquito. The dance ended, Alex brought out a platter of sliced melon with yoghurt, and George and Claire, after a polite sampling, excused themselves and went downstairs to bed.

13

GEORGE AND CLAIRE TOOK THE road in front of the hotel into town and, fifteen minutes later, turned into the south entrance of the large cruciform Municipal Market. A glaring white sunlight poured through the high glass ceiling and intricate network of metal beams, illuminating the passageways, the shops selling meats and cheeses and long tables holding vast arrays of sparkling fish and produce. *Aromata kai khromata*, Claire thought, admiring the shiny purple globes of eggplant, the pyramids of glistening red, green and orange peppers, and the clean, sweet smell of ripeness coming from the fruit stands. They bought a few peaches, exited the west segment of the cross, and walked north towards the harbor.

A labyrinth of hot close alleys, packed with tourists and laddered displays of fabric, pottery and leather handbags, led downhill to the open waterfront, where they found a table under an umbrella at the edge of one of the many cafés. They ordered water and coffee and sat in silence eating their peaches, mopping up the juice after every bite. An occasional cool breeze stirred the fringe on the umbrella above them.

"You never married," Claire said, inviting an explanation. Their drinks had come, and Claire had another mess. She put her napkin under the cup on the saucer to soak up the spilled coffee and wished she had ordered something cold.

"I never thought I'd be any good at it," George replied. "Besides I've never liked the idea of another person having to look after me. Cooking, cleaning, that sort of thing." George obviously lived in a world still observant of a sex-determined division of labor. He searched her face for a reaction. "But I will marry you if you like." He looked sincere, but Claire found the proposal insultingly arbitrary. Anyway, she had already decided that she did not want to marry again.

"And then for a long time I was studying to be a priest." He looked out at the water and the long jetty of yellowish stone. "By the time I had decided against that, I was an old bachelor of twenty-eight, set in my ways."

"Why did you leave it?" Claire found his revelation about the priesthood intriguing. It seemed to explain some things.

"I wasn't any good at that either." He smiled.

"Why not?"

"Well, for one thing, I liked too well the company of women." At this he put his hand on her thigh in mock lasciviousness, and she felt a flicker of desire. An older American couple at a nearby table gave them a disapproving look that made her feel twenty years old. "And, among other things, I found the hierarchy distasteful."

"Did you lose your faith?"

"No, but I felt the church had lost something."

"What?"

"Its mysticism maybe. Maybe it never had it—I don't know. Anyway, I objected to its formalism and imagery. Someone said the image of a god is the last obstacle to reaching him, and I believe that to be true. In any case, I think we come from and return to a far more innocent place than most religions suggest. I feel as if I'm closer to God exploring caves."

As he said this, something flashed through Claire's mind, some memory beyond retrieval, like the shadow of an unremembered dream.

"It's interesting you should say that, about formalism I mean. Recently, as I was listening to some music, I entertained the idea that *that* is God. The music. That God is form, period."

"God is not art," George said, "though that is the last hope of many agnostics. He is not a he, a she, identity, flesh, not the pyramids, not those colossal twin towers you have in New York, nor the towering twin Buddhas in Afghanistan that the Taliban have destroyed."

"Hmm." Claire thought about his words as she gazed out to another structure, the lighthouse at the end of the jetty. George explained to her that it had been originally Venetian but was rebuilt in the last century by Egyptians. The old harbor was lovely. The limestone of the breakwater, fortress and defensive walls was a soft, rosy gold, gilded not only by the morning sun, she thought, but by history, by Midas's touch. As beautiful as it was, though, she compared this harbor unfavorably to Kapsali's, which, with its simple whitewashed buildings, seemed bright and pure, unimpressed by human history, outside of time.

The water within Chania's harbor basin was silky and calm, reminding Claire of her first day in Kapsali, sitting at Eleni's café by the water. It had been the same kind of day, still and warm with an occasional breeze. Then she was struck by something. That was the day she had seen George emerge from the water, fully clothed, and she now examined his explanation that he had become water-trapped in the cave because of the high tide and had had to swim ashore. But there had not been a high tide in the bay that day. There had even been small children in the water. The water had been smooth and unbroken. Why would George lie?

He suggested they go. They still had to stop by the Ladases' gallery in the Splantzia district, which was between the harbor and the hotel, and they had promised Zoe and Harry they would be back by one.

The beach at Rethymno was long. It began at the Venetian harbor in front of the old town and stretched eastwards, where it became the site of modern development, with restaurants, multi-storied apartment blocks and hotels going on for miles. It had a fine view of the Fortezza, the sixteenth-century fortress above the old town, and many tourist amenities, including hundreds of orange, yellow and blue beach umbrellas and stacks of plastic lounges. On the palm-lined strand, below the gardens of stately old homes, were canvas-covered restaurant pavilions and stalls selling fast food, hats and souvenirs. The beach was packed with people of all ages and shapes in various stages of undress.

"Look at the multitude!" Claire made a horrified face for Zoe, who, in an orange string bikini, had already anointed herself with oil and was lying prone on the lounge.

"Crowded," Harry observed, understating the case.

"Completely spoiled," Zoe said, "but the sun's the same. Is anybody hungry?"

"Ravenous," Harry replied. "I'll fetch us some food." He looked sceptically up at the row of stalls. "Does anybody have any ideas?"

"How about souvlaki all around?" Claire suggested.

"And something cold to drink," Zoe added.

"Perfect," Harry said, taking his wallet from a canvas bag. "I'll be back."

"Let me go with you," George offered. The men started for the concessions. Claire unrolled a straw mat and sat down with their bags and towels under the shade of an umbrella. She looked over to Zoe and wondered if Harry had been moved by the revelation in the orange bikini of her perfect brown form, gleaming with oil. She hadn't paid much attention to them since George had arrived, but had taken note the day before when Harry had toasted Zoe's "plummet-measured face."

A tall woman, wearing a short denim skirt and yellow bra top, stopped a few yards in front of them, surveyed the scene, and spread out her towel. When she removed her hat, Claire was startled by the rough angularity of her face. Without removing her mini-skirt, she stretched out on the towel, face up to the sun. Behind them, two tow-headed youngsters raced by, shouting in some unidentifiable language, and accidentally kicked sand on her mat and into Zoe's hair.

"Damn," Zoe said, sitting up and looking around for the culprits. "Let's ask George when he gets back just exactly what he finds so wonderful about tourists!"

"Let's ask George what?" George asked, smiling, as he came up behind them with four cans of cold drink and some bottles of water under his arm.

"That was fast," Claire said, taking a can of Coke.

"Tourists. George, why can't you hate tourists like every other sane person on the planet?" George sat down beside Claire. He was still smiling. Zoe amused him, she knew. "Like sheep, they all flock to the same places. They have no imagination. Tell me, George, why is that?"

"Well, Zoe, you're here. Why is that?"

"Well, yes, it's a wonderful beach—or was. The crowds have ruined it. The real Crete is in the mountains. And we're here for only a couple of hours. But look at the hundreds, the thousands, who come here from all over Europe. They stay in those monolithic hotels. This is their unbelievable destination. Why wouldn't they want to go where there are fewer people, or at least more Greeks?"

Harry was back with the warm souvlaki. The grilled lamb and oregano smelled wonderful underneath the waxy wrap.

"That's part of the appeal," George said, opening a bottle of water. "Other people. People from rural areas, especially, gravitate to other people. They like a crowd. They desire immersion in the human element." He stood up to take off his shirt.

"I desire immersion this minute," Zoe cried, "in that lovely sea." She laid her unfinished souvlaki on her lounge chair, covered it with a towel, and ran for the water.

"I'll join you," Harry called after her, and hurriedly finished his lunch. "Excuse me, you two." He took long strides down to the water, plunged in, and swam in Zoe's direction. The sea did look inviting, in spite of the motley crowd splashing near the shore. Its wide blue-green strip, glossier than jade, became a cool cobalt farther out where it met the paler blue of the sky. Blue was seductive in its promise of purity and clarity, but frightening, too, she thought, standing as it did between the warmer earth colors and troublesome black.

The woman in front of them rose awkwardly from her towel and brushed sand off her forearm, at the same time sending them a rather wan smile. George smiled back, and Claire responded with a little wave. The woman didn't look well, as if she had yet to recover from a long journey. She anchored her straw hat to the ground with a rather silly-looking small purse and walked hastily down to the water's edge. The sand was too hot for bare feet. She waded into the water, still miniskirted. Claire pointed this fact out to George, and he said nothing, refusing, as usual, to share her savouring of human idiosyncrasy. He seemed to see only the similiarities among his fellow beings. This trait of his frustrated her, for she was drawn to the particular, to the surfaces of people and things.

"I've been thinking, Claire." George opened another bottle of water and drank it down at once. "There's a very pleasant cottage in a village beyond Anogeia, which an English couple own and use in the summertime. Colin Green is the karst hydrologist working on our project. They're getting a divorce, so although he's here now, she's in London. It's more convenient, and less sad, for Colin to stay close to the cave in the ski lodge with the rest of us, so the house is free. He's offered it to us if you would like to come up there."

"Sounds wonderful, but—"

"What?"

"Well, I could stay in the ski lodge perhaps."

"Too spartan," George said quickly. "Not comfortable at all. Believe me, it compares favorably only to caves. And too many men—all men. You know. Of course, I wouldn't be able to make it back to Scala— that's the name of the little village—every evening, maybe once or twice a week, but we would see more of each other than if you stayed here."

"Why couldn't you make it to the village more often? Zeno told me it's not too far from your cave."

"Well, sometimes, especially now, we have to camp in the cave. We've reached the point where we'll be so far in that it would be a waste of time to retrace our steps every day. We carry food rations, lights and sleeping bags." Claire shuddered, imagining how it would be to spend the night in such an airless, dark space.

"Think about it," George said, getting up and drawing his hand gently over her cheek. He excused himself and walked quickly in the direction of the road. Claire picked up a piece of yoghurty onion that had slipped from the souvlaki to her leg and put it in her mouth. It tasted of suntan lotion, and she spat it out. Zoe and Harry were coming up from the water.

Zoe grabbed her towel and, holding it between her chin and chest as a screen, deftly removed her wet suit bottom and replaced it with a dry one. She pointed to the empty towel in front of them. "By the way, that woman—her name is Dora—is actually a transsexual, a man in transition."

"In fact she's staying in our hotel," Harry put in. "I think she placed her towel by us because she recognized us. She's the photographer that Alex mentioned."

"She told us all about it," Zoe said. She picked up the uneaten souvlaki and lay down. "She lives in New York, and she's undergoing several surgeries. Taking hormones, too, of course. She was open about it all—very nice."

"Where's George?" Harry asked.

"Up there," Claire said, pointing to the street. "Probably for some more water. He can't seem to get enough."

"Oh, that sounds good. I've got to get something else to drink. The souvlaki was much too salty." Zoe sprang from the lounge and put on the bra top she had just removed. She grabbed her bag and hastened up the slope of sand to the road.

"It's sad," Claire said to Harry as they watched their androgynous neighbor emerge from the water, adjust the wet miniskirt, and return to her towel. She was so large, and the self-conscious mincing step only exaggerated her lanky, narrow-hipped masculinity. The humor was there, too, the gross incongruity, but the pathos was stronger.

"Yes, sad," Harry agreed. "And sort of interesting, too, I was just thinking. Especially in light of an old philosophical argument."

"What's that?"

"The one we all more or less accept. The claim that existence precedes essence. Our friend here believes herself to be a female spirit trapped in a male body. So, in her case, 'self' seems to have preceded anatomy. She's sort of beyond nature. It's almost proof of a soul. In another culture, a more primitive—or more discriminating—one, she might be deified."

That would solve the gender problem of divinity, Claire thought. She also remembered reading the theory that human gender might be found in the brain but preferred Harry's intuition of a gendered metaphysical self. He was smiling gleefully then, looking out at the sea. Engaging ideas seemed to float easily in and out of his mind. At the moment, it appeared as if he had nothing more on his mind than the sand, the sea, and the sun, whose intense heat lay heavily around them. She longed to go for a swim and wondered if she should wait for George to reappear.

Claire stood up and looked towards the concessions. There she saw George and Zoe together in a group standing around a cheese-pie stall. Zoe reached into her bag for something and handed it to George, who then separated himself from the others and, walking to the other side of the road, disappeared into the shade between two gardens. Claire decided not to wait for him and ran down the scalding sand into the water. She swam out beyond the people playing near the shore and turned on her back. Zoe had returned to the umbrella without, Claire noticed, the drink she had so desperately wanted. From the water, the holiday scene took on a more pleasant aspect. The flame of the sun seemed to weld everything together. The tawdry commerce on the street, the antique town behind it, the high rises farther down, and the bodies on the beach seemed a single shimmering thing.

Sunburnt and tired, they were back at The Daedalus around five o'clock. As they stood rather aimlessly around the lobby, waiting, Claire supposed, for someone to make further plans, George mentioned that he wasn't feeling well. She followed him up the stairs. It was just a headache, he insisted, nothing, the sun being hard on "old cave bats" like himself. He was going to have a nap, and he would be at her room at eight. There was a restaurant he wanted them to try in the Turkish quarter. Going back down the hall, she noticed Zoe just letting herself into her room.

"George mentioned a Turkish restaurant tonight. Interested?"

"Is he up to it, do you think?"

"Just a headache, he said." Zoe frowned. She looked as if she had wanted to say something but decided against it. "Want to come?"

"Don't think so, Claire. I'm exhausted. I was hoping to sleep in this morning, but Harry was at my door early, wanting to play."

"Hmm." Claire was looking into her face for signs of emotional involvement.

"Not what you think. Why don't you come in for a second?"

She followed Zoe into the room and leaned against the wardrobe, which, she noticed, was in better condition than her own. "He seems interested," Claire observed.

"I'm the one who's interested. And that's okay—*endaxi*! What's driving me crazy is he's pretending to be interested, feels sorry for me or something. God knows. Anyway, it's very awkward. We can be friends, of course. I'm not so far gone that that's not possible. In fact, I'd like that, if he'd just cut out the act. He's very amusing. We have a good time. We even discussed doing some extensive sightseeing together, maybe going to Heraklion on Friday. By the way, he's older than you think. Forty-four."

"Perhaps you should have a talk," Claire suggested, going to the door. "Look, if you change your mind about tonight, George is coming down the hall at eight. And if you see the others, tell them what we're doing."

Claire let herself into her room, which she found delightfully dim and cool. She took a shower, picked up Forster's *A Passage to India*, and climbed into bed. The book was a 1952 paperback edition, the pages stiff and yellowing into tan around their edges. She brought it to her nose. There, again, was that damp, sweet smell she liked. She began at the beginning: *Except for the Marabar Caves—and they are twenty miles off— the city of Chandrapore presents nothing extraordinary. Edged rather than washed by the river....* Amazing, she thought, how tiny lines and curves taking prescribed directions, dark print on a light page, could create a whole world, new and outrageous, where there had been none before.

Claire had fallen asleep and was aroused suddenly, as if by a noise. She was wide awake, not at all drowsy, as she normally felt after sleep. It was seven o'clock. She went to the window and saw Harry Smythe sitting below in the garden. The tall man, slightly slouched with ankle crossed over knee, looked rather uncomfortable in the small chair. He was reading a book and smoking a cigarette. It was a pleasant tableau, the man she was used to seeing in high animation now in a quiet, solitary mode. As he exhaled, his eyes left the book to follow the trail of blue smoke, as though it might lead to some interesting insight. The reflected sunlight on the upper walls of the surrounding apartment houses gave the shadowed, well-like space within the garden an isolated aspect. It seemed more like a representation of reality than reality itself, a photograph, perhaps, looked at on a cold winter's day, long after the man had gone and the garden had withered. She stayed at the window a while, staring at the Englishman reading a book in the lively, wayward Mediterranean garden.

There was the book she had been reading, peeping out from under the bed. Suddenly she wanted to talk to Harry. She tapped sharply on the window. He looked up, startled. Then he was beaming, welcoming the interruption, motioning for her to join him.

Claire took the chair Harry gave up and began to describe to him the sense of wonder she had felt beginning Forster's novel, as if those words were the first words she had ever read, but in the back of her mind was the odd encounter she had had with Zoe just then in the hallway. As she entered the corridor, there had been the sound of a door closing and Zoe coming from the direction of George's room. When Zoe saw her, she started and blushed. Then she stammered something about having heard a noise coming from that direction and going to the window at the end of the hall to check. Claire hadn't the slightest doubt she was lying, but, wanting to ease her embarrassment, replied that she, too, had been awakened abruptly, most likely by the same noise. Zoe had been to see George, she was sure. But why should Zoe lie? She was certain there was no cause for suspicion or jealousy but was, nevertheless, puzzled.

"Hmm, quite," Harry was saying in response to her words about beginning the Forster novel. "I've felt the same way about reading—and writing."

The garden had a strong geranium smell. A procession of fat black ants came from behind the upended pot on which Harry sat, its individuals carrying stick-like burdens twice their size. A bluebottle sailed between them and landed on what looked like part of a marble frieze, and from a far corner of the garden came the buzz of bees. The cat was nowhere in sight. They sat for a while in companionable silence.

"Do you remember mentioning an article you had read about why we sleep?" Harry asked. "And that they'd found no answer, really, except that oscillation is simply the way biology works. They couldn't get beyond that. They'd come to a wall." Harry took a cigarette from a pack lying with his book on the ground and lit it.

"May I have one?"

"Sorry." He stood up and, withdrawing another cigarette from the pack, crossed the distance between them. He put it in her mouth and stood close, lighting it for her, protecting the flame from a non-existent breeze.

"It's pleasant here," she remarked languidly, feeling, for some reason, like a character in a Chekhov play. "A little cooler." She had felt a slight sexual stirring as Harry lit her cigarette. How good it was to feel again.

"Where was I?" Harry asked, sitting down again, this time on a stack of stone pavers. "Oh, I know, the wall. Science. Well, I was thinking maybe there's nothing beyond that. I got to thinking about language and the way it works. How it bifurcates everything, how it exists in oppositions—the famous dance of 'binary opposites.' And so the theorists talk about text having no fixed meaning and that sort of thing."

The cat had appeared and was slinking back and forth against Harry's legs. He unconsciously stroked it. "Some say language is an arbitrary organization of the world and blinds us to reality, but I tend to think it reveals it, even at its core. Look at the double helix of DNA and particles and waves."

"Yes, and sleep and wakefulness, a 'dialectic of life' you called it in Potamos. And the something out of nothing—suddenly Miss Quested and Dr. Aziz in Chandrapore. A miracle of creation!"

"Aren't you lovely," Harry said, giving her a wide smile. Harry could make that kind of remark in such a detached way that the words dissolved as soon as they were spoken, alleviating embarrassment or the need for a response. He had an attractive lightness about him that belied, or perhaps proved, his intellect. "By the way, how's George doing?"

"He's sleeping now. We're having a Turkish dinner tonight. Would you like to come."

"Zoe said that he's not feeling well." Harry picked up the cat and placed him on his thigh, from which it took a grand leap and ran into a shrub.

"He'll be fine." Claire checked her watch. It was almost seven-thirty. She wondered if George had an alarm clock.

"It seems you're very much in love. A good man, George." Harry rested his elbows on his knees and, head down, contemplated the burning cigarette he held between them.

"Yes."

Claire heard an insect whine. The wretched mosquitoes were starting, and she reacted allergically to bites. She pulled a cylinder of repellent stick that she was never without from her shorts pocket and applied it to her legs, arms, and face. Harry watched the procedure closely. "It's really rather strange," Claire said. "I'm in love with something, I mean someone I can't quite comprehend. He's so—large. We don't talk much. He seems somehow to be beyond that—you know, conversation. What we're doing now. Maybe it has to do with what you were just saying about language. Its split quality, its 'thisness' or 'thatness.' For him, everything's connected."

"A mark of genius, someone said, can't remember who. One of our British literary icons no doubt. 'Intelligence perceives differences, genius unity,' something like that. It seems as if that is what you're looking for."

"Unity?"

"Yes. Simplicity, purity, or something of that sort."

"You know, as I was floating in the water today and looking back to the beach with the sun crashing down on the scene—everything was blurred. It was the way I used to see things as a child, before my parents discovered I was near-sighted and needed glasses. From my vantage-point in the water, things had lost their separateness. It looked like a vast impressionistic painting. Something was holding it all together. It was beautiful."

Harry looked at her for a long time, saying nothing. Then he checked his watch and rose. "I think you'd better go fetch George."

A fully recovered George and Claire dined by themselves, after which they sat on a bench in a small park near the seawall. The bright moon was doing its usual wondrous things to the water, scattering a fountain of stars on the silky black liquid and, farther out, stunning it into a motionless crust of hammered silver. A fisherman dragged his small caïque ashore and, sitting on the ground in a pool of lamplight, began to caulk a leak with a burner and paraffin. They watched him as they made their plans. George would take a bus up to Anogeia on Tuesday afternoon and be back in the cave on Wednesday. They decided that if Zoe and Harry did leave for Heraklion on Friday, Claire would then take the bus to Anogeia. George would meet her there and, together, they would go to Scala and move into the cottage for an indefinite period, perhaps for even as long as George was needed at the cave.

14

CLAIRE LIKED THE MOUNTAIN village of Scala at once. It was small, verdant and situated on a river. George parked the jeep at the square across from the taverna, where they were to meet the man who looked after Colin's cottage in his absence. The Scala square was not a formal one. In fact, it wasn't a square at all, but an irregular triangle, bound by the back wall of a small church, a stone parapet running diagonally from the road along a creek bed, and the road itself. Tables and red plastic chairs belonging to the taverna sat at intervals along the church wall and the parapet, and the area was shaded by an enormous plane tree.

Claire sat down while George went inside the taverna to look for Manolis, who he had been told worked there and lived in a room above it. The building was old and plain, a two-storied white block with dark green shutters and, the only note of grace, a grilled, narrow-ledged balcony in front of French doors on the second floor, directly above the single door of the entrance. There were hundreds of similar structures all over southern Europe, facing squares everywhere. Claire had always dreamed of living in such a place, in the center of a small town, and being able, in fits of restlessness, to walk through the long windows to the ledge and gaze down on the activity below, joining it if so inspired. She now imagined that this was somehow related to the subject-object thing that Zoe had talked about. Standing on a balcony above a busy square had the obvious advantage of seeing before being seen.

The French doors flew open, and Claire saw George and Manolis, a handsome young man, dishevelled from sleep and smoking a cigarette. They waved, and George spread the fingers of one hand, indicating they would be five minutes. She stood up and looked over the parapet. There was a drop of about twelve feet to the creek bed, which was a tributary of the main river on the edge of town, and, along it, a stone trough. On the opposite bank was a tree-lined path and the back walls of several dwellings with small curtained windows, utility porches strung with clotheslines, and stairs to the ground.

The men appeared, and Manolis, speaking English with an Australian accent, assured Claire that she could rely on him if she needed anything in George's absence, adding that he had a telephone in the taverna and the number of the ski lodge near the cave. Then Claire and George got back into the jeep with Manolis and started back in the direction from which they had come. The village was quiet. Other than Manolis, they had seen no one except for two black-shrouded old women, one sitting in the doorway of her cottage and another leaning over her terrace wall, brushing something away with a short-handled broom. They came to an imposing church with another bell tower, turned left, crossed a bridge over the riverbed, and passed a small market and several houses. Then they were in front of their cottage, the last building on the rural road, but still just a short walk from the square.

The cottage was made of stone, left unplastered, and it had a dead-center front door with shuttered windows on each side of it. It was the essential house, a child's crayon rendering. A mass of colorful flowers—hollyhocks, roses, lilies and daisies—grew between it and the road, and Manolis had tended the garden well. He had also prepared for their arrival. The house was clean, and, on a heavy low table in the sitting room, next to a bowl of fresh daisies, sat a plate of *koularakia* and plums. The main room was beautiful, with its exposed stone walls, wide-mouthed corner fireplace and plain furnishings. Rush-seated chairs surrounded a red handwoven rug, and a rack displaying blue and white crockery hung on the wall. Under the rack was a utility table with a few copper pots, an earthenware casserole, and other items, overflow from the small kitchen, which was to the left off the sitting room through an angled door. Open stairs led to a loft bedroom and a bath above.

Manolis left, promising them lamb chops at the taverna that evening, and Claire inspected the kitchen. The young man had neglected the refrigerator. It was grimy, with yellow bits of ancient vegetables and smears of tomato sauce, and on the top shelf a carton of putrid milk, a jar of tahini, and a cracked plastic measuring cup with instant coffee that had become paste. Claire looked at her watch. They would have time for a nap before returning to the village.

At dusk Claire awoke to an unfamiliar white mist, the filmy swath of mosquito netting encircling the bed and softening the edges of the room—the rough beams in the ceiling, the carved wooden dove on the thick, deep windowsill, the lantern on a table under the window. It made more gradual the transition from sleep to consciousness. Birth should occur in the dark, or, at least, in a dimly lit room. A cave, she thought, remembering the birthplace of Zeus and, in the Greek version, of Christ.

She looked over to George, the man who slept in caves, still asleep on his side, facing her with one hand under his head and the other on the sheet reaching towards her. Helpless, innocent, doomed, she thought, and felt the pang of humanity's shared helplessness and innocence, the shared doom. Her love for George seemed to be awakening her to a more ideal, more generalized love. "Even for tourists," she said aloud, smiling, wanting George to wake up.

"What?" He opened his eyes.

"I even love, well, tourists—maybe."

"And why is that?"

"Because I love you." She picked up his hand and kissed the palm. "*S'agapo*."

"What?"

"In Greek. 'I love you' in Greek."

"Ooh. *S'agapo*. Beautiful sounds."

"I'm hungry."

"Well, it *is* about dinnertime. Let's go and see what kind of cook Manolis is. I'm hungry, too, and we have to shop before."

They rose early the next morning, ate some figs from a tree behind the house, and were back in the jeep, climbing the narrow, winding road towards George's cave. Above the tree line, the terrain took on an eerie, unnatural look. It was as if the ground in every direction, and as far as the eye could see, had been laminated with rock, the surface of which was splintered along its striations into an almost symmetrical grid of narrow cracks. George told her that the broken surface was called "scree" and explained the karstic phenomenon, the erosion of limestone by water and carbon dioxide.

"When will we see your cave?" They were not going as far as the cave, but to a place where they could see it from a distance. George had brought binoculars for that purpose.

"That's another forty minutes or so up the road, but before that we're stopping for breakfast."

"A taverna?"

"No." George seemed amused by something.

"Where?"

"You'll see." They rode in silence. Sheep and goats were grazing everywhere, and their bells made a sweet music.

"What are the animals eating?" Claire asked, unable to imagine their finding anything to eat on the naked rock.

"Salad. A fine one, too. Full of iron and vitamins. This is their summer pasture. In late autumn, they'll return to their folds in the villages." Near the road, a rather coarse and inedible-looking tuft of gray-green was being routed from a crack in the rock by a beautifully horned goat.

"A kri-kri," George said, "the indigenous wild goat." He was pulling the jeep to the side of the road.

"Why are we stopping?"

"Breakfast."

"Here?"

"Follow me."

They crossed the road, and George led Claire over a rise and down towards a hut, an irregular semi-sphere of shale, which was almost indistinguishable from the rocky ground around it. There was a shout of greeting, and a dark grizzled man in high boots and an old woollen suit-jacket approached them. He leaned his crook against the hut and embraced George. George introduced him to Claire in Greek and then asked a question she couldn't understand. "Of course," the man called Panyiottis said in English.

George drew her into the hut through its small front door. It was dark and smelled of smoke, damp wool and dung. In the center of the dirt floor were the remains of a fire and, on a wide ledge jutting from the wall, a bed of dried herbs and old blankets. Leaning next to the bed was a shotgun. Another small door opened outside to a tiny, low-walled space where some cooking and serving utensils were strewn on several stacks of shale. The shepherd was puttering in this little side yard, which served as a kitchen and dairy. He cut some hard black bread and gave them each a hunk of it, encouraging them to dip it in a bowl of water to soften. Then he ushered them outside, pointing to two flat rocks nearby where they could sit, and returned to his kitchen. Soon Panyiottis appeared with a large bowl of yogurt and two smaller bowls and spoons. He perched on another rock and, eyes glittering with pleasure, watched them eat. When they had finished, they stood up and thanked their host, and he escorted them back to the road. Before they got into the jeep, Panyiottis wordlessly took Claire's hand and embraced George.

"I shall never forget that. Thank you," Claire said to George when they were on their way again. "How do you know him?"

"Colin introduced us. It was actually Panyiottis who discovered our cave while tending his flocks above here. It was late summer, about this time last year, when he noticed a dark gap in the mountain he hadn't seen before. Luckily, he contacted the right people, and the government immediately put it off-limits. Anyway, now he feels a proprietary interest in the project, and whenever he sees one of our jeeps he flags it down and insists on sharing some of his food. His rabbit cooked over a thyme fire is delicious. Last week Colin and I took him up to the cave just so he could see what's going on."

"Here we are," George announced as he brought the jeep to a halt and reached into the glove compartment for the binoculars. They walked up the road and turned into a donkey track, which took them down into a flume and then upwards towards a high ridge. After thirty minutes of strenuous hiking, they reached the top. George handed Claire the glasses. The sun was high, and its reflection off the bald rock had been intense. She took a bandana from her pack and wiped her forehead. Then she put the binoculars to her eyes, and George turned her in the right direction.

"Oh, now I see it!" By then she had seen a number of caves and was surprised by her own excitement. Through the glasses, the dark yawn in the mountain stood out, as though it were alive, the only living thing against the dead rock. "And you say it was actually hidden by a single boulder? It must have been immense."

"Look a bit to the left and down."

"Oh yes, there it is."

George embraced her from behind and put his mouth to her ear. "So now you know where I am, Clairaki."

"Yes, but I would like to go there. Right up to it, into it."

"And I want to take you. But tomorrow I have to return alone. We're getting to work straight away. Perhaps next time." A sudden and bewildered look passed over his face.

"George! What's wrong?"

He let himself down slowly on a rock.

"Too much sun, I'm afraid. Thirsty, and I forgot to bring water."

"I have some." Claire quickly rooted through her pack, found the half-empty bottle, and thrust it at him. He drank it down quickly. She was upset. He was never without that silly first-aid kit, and then he forgot something as essential as water. She remembered Zoe's saying that he was careless. "Perhaps we should go back to the car now. Can you make it?"

"You go ahead," George said. "I'll catch up."

"No."

"Please, I'll be right with you."

Later that afternoon, Manolis unlocked the door of the twelfth-century church by the square and turned on a light. George and Claire circled the interior, trying to make out the figures on the fading frescoed walls. On the iconostasis was another madonna. This one, under an opaque yellow hat of a halo, had a face, but her features were so perfect and formalized as to be characterless. Perhaps it is the transparency of symmetry that draws us to beauty, Claire thought, that in fact defines it. It is self-cancelling and therefore doesn't come between us and—and what? A question for Byron Velisarios, should she ever see him again.

"I just remembered a bizarre dream I had on my first day in Chania," Claire confided. "Maybe it was seeing your cave this afternoon, and now this icon. I dreamt they were the same thing. Or, rather, in my dream, the black face of the madonna in Kythera became the mouth of a cave."

"Dreams," George said noncommittally and turned to the exit. "Let's not keep Manolis any longer. He has to get ready for the crowd." A tour bus was expected to stop in town that evening, a weekly event, before returning to Anogeia and Rethymno. They had passed it earlier that afternoon on their way back to Scala. George dropped some drachmas in the offertory, thanked Manolis, and they set out for a stroll around the village. The shopkeepers were opening their stores a little earlier so they could have their street displays out in time for the arrival of the bus. Large and colorful plastic oil containers, strung together through their handles, were hung outside one shop and looked as festive as balloons. The square itself had become a market for a vibrant array of textiles, woven by women of the village from the wool of their own sheep, exhibiting patterns that had been repeated there for centuries.

They took the steps down to the creek bed and followed it until another set of steps led them back up to an unfamiliar road. Moving away from the center of the village, they were soon in the outskirts. The houses were farther apart and there was a scattering of wooden outbuildings. One dim, hay-strewn shed contained a braying donkey, another a potter's wheel and stacks of jars. The clay gave off a cool scent as they passed. Most were full of farm implements and stores of grain, oil and wine. It was still siesta time, and they saw no one on the road until a kerchiefed middle-aged woman suddenly appeared, closing a garden gate behind her. She had gathered something in the skirt of her apron and, seeing them, looked down and scurried away. Poaching fruit, George surmised, adding that some of the village houses were empty at that time of year.

They returned to the square and sat down at a table between two rug displays, knowing that dinner would be an impossibility until the tourists had gone. At least from there they could see the bus arrive and watch the goings-on. George pulled a folded piece of paper from his pocket and spread it open on the table. It was a sketch of what, at first glance, Claire took to be a land mass. But if the narrow-necked circular protrusions from the main body had been on earth, they would have broken off ages before into the sea. It was the cave, looking like the foetus of some fantastical creature.

"Is this all of it?"

"All that we know of now. This is merely the shape of it. The conditions and contents of the galleries and all the elevations are on the actual chart. But you can see the entrance here. These are the antechambers, and here is a lake. We've crossed that already."

"How?"

"Boats—inflatable dinghies. Because there's water in it, we call the cave 'active.' And that's why we must probe as far as we can before the rainy season. Now, these round protrusions are chambers that lead nowhere else. And here *we* are." He took out a pen and drew an *X*. "We've been gradually climbing, but now we're approaching a steep shaft that may go down a hundred metres or more."

"Hmm. Not at all like the Marabar Caves."

"What?"

"A book I'm rereading. *A Passage to India*. Have you read it? There are these caves."

"Yes, I did read the novel years ago in school. And, of course, I remember the caves if nothing else. I wouldn't be surprised if that book had something to do with what I'm doing now. Excuse me, I'm going to get some water. What would you like?"

"Some retsina, maybe some feta and onions." George crossed the street to the taverna, and, as he entered the building, the tour bus came into town and stopped just short of the square. Claire watched as the tourists came off the bus, either singly or in pairs. They weren't a bad-looking group. She supposed it was the more adventurous or curious ones who left the beach areas and came up to the mountains, or they simply looked better with more clothes on. Or maybe she really was softening under George's influence. A woman wearing five-inch high-heels and a camera around her neck stepped down. Claire was thinking how uncomfortable the shoes must be when she realized it was the transsexual from Rethymno beach. Dora teetered into the taverna with some fellow passengers while the rest began to either explore the town or examine the rugs and embroidered linens surrounding Claire on the square. George returned, followed by Manolis with the drinks and *meze*. The mountains behind the town were black against the pink sky, and it was beginning to get cool. Once the bus left, they would find another table inside the taverna, as they had done the night before.

"Does your cave have an echo?" Claire asked, offering George a piece of cheese.

"An echo?"

"Yes. Remember the Marabar Caves did. Mrs. Moore thought it was terrible because no matter what the original sound, the echo was the same—sort of a dull boom. That knowledge changed her drastically. It may even have killed her. After visiting one of the caves, she felt that no matter what happened, it amounted to nothing more than 'boum.'"

"'Nothing attaches.'"

"That's right. Forster's very words."

"The only ones I remember."

"I think that's why the narrator thought the caves were extraordinary—the nothingness or unseenness of them."

"Most caves are unseen," George said. Yes, Claire thought, just as the number of dead exceeds that of the living and the dark matter of space is greater than the light.

"Speaking of extraordinary, did you see Dora inside?"

"Dora?"

"You remember the woman I was telling you about—the one at the beach—or the man who's becoming a woman? Oh, there she is, coming out of the taverna. I think she sees us. She's coming over. She looks as if she's going to fall over those shoes any second." Claire gave Dora a smile of welcome as she approached their table.

"You're Claire Paxton, aren't you? We haven't actually met. I'm Dora Hutts, from your hotel. We saw each other at the beach, and I talked to your friends?"

"Oh, yes. Would you like to sit down?" George rose and pulled up another chair.

"Oh, no, not now, thank you. You see I would like to stay here a few days, have a look around and take some photographs, but I have to find a room. I need to talk to the taverna man. But I have a message for you from Zoe Stefanides. I was going to leave it inside the taverna, but now that I've seen you—." She opened her purse, pulled out a postcard, and handed it to Claire. It was Zoe's handwriting on the back of a photographic postcard showing the Cretan goat. *Friday. Claire—H. and I (all is fine in that regard) are leaving for Heraklion. Coming to Scala on way back next week, maybe Tues. H. wants to see mountains. Great postal service, isn't it? Z.*

"Good news. Thank you, Dora, very much. Are you sure you won't—?"

"No, thank you, honey. Maybe some other time. Manolis is waiting." Dora tripped across the square and re-entered the taverna.

15

THE JEEP STIRRED UP A SPIRAL of dust, a smudge against the flat blue sky, before it turned into the main road. Church bells were clamoring in the village, the insistent and prolonged ringing that told of a function, a sound that would actually bring people to morning worship, unlike the purely ritualistic ringing of church bells in urban places. The dust settled, and Claire went back into the house. George had taken all his belongings. There were no reminders, things to care for, emblems of him. She felt a terrible emptiness as she stood and looked around the room. The daisies that Manolis had cut from the garden were already withering, but she had no desire to replace them.

Claire had not felt this desolation at their first separation when George had left Kythera for Crete. But there she had had friends and acquaintances. She thought longingly of Kapsali, swimming at the little cove, the Greek lessons with Eleni, the seaside cafés, the Ladases, Zoe, Harry. Perhaps coming to the mountain village had been a mistake. Maybe coming to Crete period. Now she considered the possibility that the few hours she had spent with George, no matter how satisfying, could not compensate for the bleak and lonely days ahead. In Scala she had no one, not even a routine, nor was there anything she particularly wanted to do. George had not known when he would be back. If he had given her a date, she might at least have found a calendar and begun crossing out the days. Some sense of accomplishment in that—living through a prescribed period, progressing from one day to the next. She considered returning to Chania for a time but then remembered that Zoe and Harry were not there. Only the Ladases, and they were busy every day at the gallery. Fortunately, Zoe and Harry might be coming to Scala on Tuesday, just a couple of days away. Perhaps she could persuade them to stay a while. Looking around the sitting room, she wondered where Harry might sleep. Zoe could sleep upstairs with her. But until then, what?

Claire had given up on her Eleni story, not knowing where to take it. She abandoned it at the point Eleni had given up dreams of Carlo, was hopelessly infatuated with Kostas, and was being pursued by Aleko, whom she despised. But Eleni must marry Aleko. That was fact. Life had served up that mystery to solve. Why had that happened? A change of heart? Not likely. Her virgin marriage testified to that. Arranged by parents, by anxious mothers? Again, not likely. Arranged marriages were rare by that time, and money could not have entered into it, for a dowry, had there been one, would not have been significant. Claire had put the story away, out of sight, hoping that if she removed herself from it for a while, something would come to mind. But no solution had come. She walked up the stairs and fell into bed, desiring nothing but oblivion.

She awoke at eleven, feeling better, and decided she would simply have to animate herself, establish a routine that would give her life a daily purpose and meaning. Yes, a routine was essential. She would walk into the village now, eat something at the taverna, buy postcards to send to California, and stop at the market on the way home before it closed. Then she would acquaint herself with the kitchen, perhaps even make something. That would become her daily routine—postcards, groceries, and a meal, alternating between lunch at the taverna one day and dinner there the next. Although she needed to go to Scala, she didn't want to be there too much since she would be conspicuous in such a village. Claire showered, put on a long skirt, a loose bare top and her daypack.

Before leaving the house, she took the wilting daisies to the kitchen, removed the flowers, and, turning the bowl over to empty the water, realized there had never been any. Manolis had forgotten it. She filled the bowl with water, replaced it on the table in the sitting room, and looked around for some secateurs. Once in the garden, she decided to leave the hollyhocks alone. It had taken them too long to get to their present height. To cut them would be, in a lesser way, like picking the chartreuse bloom off the aloe she had seen in Kythera, the bloom the plant had struggled for fifteen years to produce. She settled for some more daisies, a single lily, and some glossy green leaves from a shrub. After arranging them in the bowl and feeling better for having accomplished that small task, she set out for town.

The air was thick and heavy with a moisture that was uncharacteristic of Greece at that time of year, and it was difficult to walk quickly. She turned into the market to find out when it closed for the afternoon. The perspiring, bald proprietor was on a ladder, stacking things on a shelf. The store was well-stocked with household and packaged goods and had a refrigerated case for milk, cheese and yogurt, but his produce, displayed on tables outside the shop in a roofed but otherwise unenclosed area, was scanty and old. Claire picked up a bunch of beets with yellow tops, some sprouting potatoes, a couple of over-ripe, cracked tomatoes in a swarm of gnats, some onions, and a handful of bruised apricots. Putting them on the counter, she asked the man to hold them for her return. He had seen her reaction to the produce and assured her, as she left his shop, that there would be fresh fruits and vegetables on Tuesday.

She stopped for a while at the beginning of the bridge in the dappled shade of some spindly oleander bushes growing from the banks of the riverbed. She stood very still so as to catch any breeze that might come up. None had, so she crossed the bridge and turned into the main road. There she stepped up her pace, looking forward to sitting under the generous shade of the tree in the square. It was Sunday and, as she entered the village, well-groomed people who had been to church were going in and out of the shops.

Claire entered the dark taverna. It would be even cooler sitting there at a table in front of the rotating fan than outside under the tree. The room was a green, high-ceilinged space with a large unframed mirror and numerous images on the walls—a magazine photo of a Cézanne in a cheap, ornate frame, posters of Lenin, Stalin, Che Guevara and

Marilyn Monroe, two portrait-studio photos of local politicians, and a framed advertisement for Papastratos cigarettes. Manolis was behind the counter, polishing glassware, and Claire ordered a tomato salad and beer. The television was on, a news program from Athens. Claire listened but was still far from understanding Greek spoken at a normal speed.

A fat, pony-tailed priest and two middle-aged men entered the taverna and took seats against the wall. They lit cigarettes and sat in silence to watch the news. At a table near hers, two old men were engaged in conversation. They were as bent and fissured as the mountains they had lived in all their lives and wore woollen jackets and caps, in spite of the heat. One dangled a cane and a plastic bag of oranges between his legs. When Manolis brought Claire's food, they became aware of her presence and stared at her with some hostility. The taverna, in their time, had been solely the domain of men. She had anticipated arousing that kind of unfriendly curiosity in a town that saw tourists mainly when they came in on buses, and then only for short periods of time. She had gone from being the observer in Kythera to the one being observed.

"There you are, honey." Dora Hutts, again in five-inch heels, was aimed in her direction. Claire remembered then her saying she was going to be around for a while. God, she wanted company, but—. "May I sit down?" she asked, taking a seat before Claire could respond.

"Sure. Take off those shoes and stay a while." Claire had finished her salad, so she lit a cigarette and offered Dora one. What would they ever talk about? Claire was disoriented. Was she talking to a woman or a man? The confusion brought home to her how gender-based ordinary conversation was. And how did Dora regard her? Was she a "sister," or was there some vestige of masculinity that saw her as "other"?

"I think I will. No, not a cigarette—I'm going to eat something. I meant take off these shoes. They're killing me!" Some knee movement under the table indicated she was doing just that, but her eyes did not leave Claire's face. Claire looked away. "Oh, Manolis." Dora raised her arm. "Another salad here, please." The priest and his companions against the wall looked over to Dora. They were saying something to each other and snickering. They knew. The old men also looked around, but only for a moment, and then went back to their conversation. To them, Dora was just another woman invading their territory.

"Where's your friend?" Dora asked.

"Oh, George. Well, he's—" Where should she begin? Make it short and to the point, she told herself, not wanting a prolonged conversation. The more she said, the more space there would be for Dora to lay claim. "George is a cave explorer, and he's doing that right now, farther up the mountain." She would not tell her he had gone for an indefinite period. There was something blatantly needy about Dora, and Claire wasn't interested in her friendship.

"Oh, men and their mountains." Dora smiled sadly and shook her head. "Honey, we play second fiddle to those mountains. Trust me, I know." Claire began to feel a little more at ease. Dora was relating to her woman-to-woman. If she could just forget what was under the skirt.

"Do you have a boyfriend?" Claire ventured the question, thinking why not? Go for broke. Manolis brought Dora her salad, and they exchanged some pleasantries.

"Pardon me, dearie. You asked me something?"

"A boyfriend?" She now felt the inanity of the question. The fan was blowing her hair in her face, and she sidled her chair a few inches away.

"Many!" Dora laughed without amusement. "Girlfriends, too. I'm pan-sexual." Her expression became serious as she watched Manolis walk up to the television and change the channel. Claire studied her face. She had on a heavy make-up base, lipstick and false eyelashes, which, besides looking ludicrous, accentuated the masculine angles of her face. "Beggars can't be choosers, and the market isn't very wide for a girl like me. I have to take what I can get. But, like most women," she said, turning back to Claire, "I'm looking for a good man and a monogamous relationship." She reached into her tiny purse, the one Claire remembered from Rethymno beach, and brought out a package of cigarettes. "Someone straight. But I can't hope for that until I have some more surgery. Would you like to hear about my surgeries?"

"Uh, no thanks. I'm a little squeamish." Claire was looking for an exit line. She looked at her watch. Then she remembered, gratefully, the groceries she had to pick up. Dora reached across the table for Claire's lighter and lit her cigarette.

"But surgery is wonderful, honey. It's fantastic to be just an object— you know, to be cosseted and fussed over. And then the wonderful languor of slipping into anesthesia, into delicious dark—just like that."

"I'm afraid of the dark," Claire said.

Dora, not hearing her, brought the long, thin fingers of one hand together and then sprang them open like a flower. "Just letting go. Believe me, surgery is underrated."

"I'm sure it is. Look, Dora, maybe we can do this again. But I have to get to the store before it closes." Claire stood up and put some drachmas on the table.

Dora looked disappointed, but also resigned, as if the sight of people hurrying away from her was something she had grown used to. She smiled and waved as Claire left the taverna. There was definitely something about her Claire liked, beyond the pity. She thought it might have to do with courage.

It was daybreak, and Claire woke up in the cloud of mosquito netting, feeling a hot, vague discomfort. She had been dreaming about being on a mountain and buzzed by small planes. Then she realized she was itching and unable to open one eye. Feeling her way through the net and into the bathroom, she stood at the mirror and was shocked by the reflection, a sickening distortion of her face. One eye, except for a narrow, glaucous slit was covered with a swollen pad of skin. The inside of her upper lip was swollen almost to her nose, and one nostril of her nose was twice the size of the other. An earlobe had also doubled in size, and where things were less disastrous, on her neck, chest, and arms, there were large red bumps. Obviously, the mosquitoes had found a hole somewhere in the net. They had had a feast.

Claire groped around in one of her plastic kits for a mosquito stick and applied it furiously everywhere. The sting and sharp alcohol smell was soothing. She felt nauseated and remembered she had some antihistamines but realized she was going to need something much stronger. Knowing she would have to go into Scala, she checked her watch. Seven. Good. By the time she dressed and walked there, Manolis would be up and, she hoped, a doctor as well— if there was one. She hurriedly put on the skirt of the day before, a T-shirt and her daypack. She found her spare, outmoded sunglasses with the oversized lenses, remembered the large straw hat on a hook by the kitchen door, and set out, walking as quickly as she could.

Just past the church, Claire saw an old woman sitting by her front door, trimming artichokes. Perhaps she wouldn't need Manolis after all. Removing her sunglasses for a moment, she approached the woman and asked where the doctor lived. The woman made some alarmed, sympathetic sounds and stood up from her chair. Then speaking rapidly in Greek, she pointed up the outside stairs to the second story of her house and sat Claire down in her chair. Claire guessed she hadn't understood. Or, more likely, she had understood and was going to apply a home remedy. Claire began to protest and repeated her pleas for a doctor. Yes, yes, the woman said adamantly in English and pointed upstairs again. Claire couldn't believe she had actually happened upon a doctor's house.

The woman took the stairs and, after a few minutes, summoned Claire. At the top was a broad, sunny terrace, off which were two rooms. The second door was open, and she motioned Claire inside. To her surprise, it was a doctor's office. She took the chair next to the cot, and the woman left, indicating she would be back in a few minutes. When she returned, she was smiling proudly and had a young man, presumably the doctor, in tow. He greeted Claire in English and bid goodbye to the woman, who seemed to want to stay and watch.

"I guess I came to the right place," Claire said. "Lucky. She was the first person I saw as I came into the village." She removed her sunglasses again and knew that words were no longer necessary.

"Mosquitoes," he said. He was short and fair and wore glasses. He approached her in the gentle, tentative way physicians have and tilted her chin upwards to examine her face.

"Accurate diagnosis," Claire said.

"Anywhere else?"

"Mainly what you see." She held out her arms. "On my chest too. They didn't get to my legs. By that time, they were glutted."

"You should be more careful. Do you use a repellent?"

"Yes, normally, but my bed has netting, and I haven't been bothered. The nights have been breezy."

"Yes, but not last night. How do you feel? I mean do you feel sick."

"Yes."

"You are allergic. I'm going to give you a shot to help the itching and also some pills and a topical cream. Then I want you to go home and rest." He ushered her to the cot and asked her to lie down on her stomach. He was busy at his cabinets. "Where are you staying?"

"At an Englishman's house—Colin Green."

"Oh, yes, I know the house," he said approaching with the needle and indicating where he was going to inject. She lifted her skirt. As he administered the shot, to distract her she thought, he advised using repellent again and suggested she buy an electric fan to discourage mosquitoes on still nights. Claire remembered that she had seen one in a cupboard in the cottage.

"Do you live here?"

"Yes. I'm here for a year," he said, dabbing the spot with disinfectant. He moved over to the sink. "I'm from Athens."

"I mean do you live here, in this house?"

"Yes, downstairs. The lady owns the house and rents a room to me and these rooms to the government."

Claire slid off the table and returned to the chair. The doctor was at his cabinets, his back to her, opening and closing drawers. Finally, he handed her a piece of paper, on which he had written some instructions in an exotic mix of English and Greek. He also gave her a vial of pills and a small tube of cortisone cream. He charged her the equivalent of ten dollars for the shot, nothing for the medications, and told her to return if there were any problems.

Back at the cottage, she rechecked her monster face in the mirror and hoped that Zoe and Harry would be delayed, preferring not to be seen until the swelling had gone down. She would isolate herself until that happened. At least now she had a mission: to rest and treat the bites. In a few days they would ooze and scab, and it would take more than a week for them to disappear. Fortunately, she had enough food and books, and she considered picking up the writing again. She undressed and stepped into the square, shallow well in the bathroom which served as a shower. The coolness of the tepid water was a relief on the bites. Afterwards, she gathered up the useless mosquito netting, tucking it behind the headboard, straightened up the bedsheets, and went back down the stairs.

In the kitchen she ate a fig and a small carton of yogurt, picked up a glass and two large bottles of water, and returned to the bedroom. There, on the bedside table, she set up a pile of books in the order of their appeal to her, along with pens and tablets. Not bad, she thought. Here she would stay until her friends arrived.

It was dusk on the same day. Claire had read several poems from the Larkin book she had borrowed from the hotel in Chania, reread some of Forster's descriptions of the Marabar Caves, and begun an engaging Fay Weldon paperback, belonging to the cottage. Then she had slept for a while. It was now approaching mosquito time. She lit a coil, diligently spread repellent over her entire body, and replaced the lantern on the table under the window with the fan, plugging it in for later. The air was hot, humid and still. She would go downstairs, boil a few potatoes, and make a small salad for dinner. Still upstairs, she heard the front door open.

"Claire—Claire, honey, it's me!" Oh, no. Dora. What an intrusion, she thought as she descended the steps.

"I hope you didn't bring your camera," Claire said, presenting herself.

"Well, well, well. Look at you. You make me look pretty good!" She had an armload of bags. Claire was glad to see she was wearing slacks and a comfortable-looking pair of flat shoes. She looked more feminine. "I've brought you dinner. Go back up those stairs, honey, and get into bed. Aunty Dora is going to take care of you." Oh dear, Claire thought, but still how kind of her. Obviously, the word had spread. She got back into bed, finding it somewhat comforting to take orders. Several minutes later, Dora appeared at the top of the stairs with a tumbler of red wine. "The best medicine," she said, handing the glass to Claire. "Now, Manolis' moussaka is still warm. Shall I make it hot, or do you like it 'luke'?"

"Warm is fine. Is there enough for you?"

"Sure. We're going to have ourselves a sweet little dinner for two. Start your wine. I'll be back in a minute."

Dora reappeared holding a tray with napkins, utensils, and two plates of the eggplant. She handed the tray to Claire and efficiently spread a paper napkin between it and her chin. Then she drew up a straight chair for herself. "Cheers," she said, raising her glass. "God, it's hot."

"Why don't we turn on the fan? I meant to do it before, to discourage the bugs."

Dora put her plate on the edge of the bed and played with the fan adjustments. Back in her chair, she was scrutinizing Claire's face and shaking her head in sympathy. "When will George be back?"

"Not too soon, I hope. I'd hate to have him see me like this. He really didn't know when. It depends on what happens at the cave, of course. I do have friends coming in a few days. Zoe and Harry. You might have read their postcard."

"Honey, I never read others' mail. Not even postcards."

They ate in silence. The only sound was the buzz of the fan as it sent its gentle breeze around the room. "More wine?" Dora asked.

"Yes, please. The moussaka is good. Please tell Manolis I'll pay him when I see him."

"No, dearie. Dinner is on me. Now I'll get the rest of the wine and our dessert." She picked up the tray and hurried down the stairs, coming up a few minutes later with the bottle and an array of biscuits on a plate. Claire was touched by Dora's kindness, more so because she knew that she had to have suffered terribly. She boldly asked her when it was she realized that she was actually female.

"Let me ask you," Dora countered. "When did *you* realize?" Claire, then understanding the absurdity of her question, blushed and looked away. She was getting tired again. The bites had given her the symptoms of flu.

"But now that I think of it," Dora said, "there was a point when I became aware of both my femaleness and my attraction to men. It was summer, and I was six or seven years old. My mother was still forcing me to have a nap every day, more for her than for me." Dora laughed. "I was the kid from hell, and I had her flummoxed. She was a conventional woman, and although I drove her crazy doing boy kinds of stuff—falling out of trees, peeing in the garden, bringing dirt and bugs into the house—what was worse for her was that she knew she had a weird one on her hands. I loved dolls, the old parental terror, and hung around my mother a lot, especially when she was at her dressing table. I was fascinated by the mirror, one of those round art deco jobs, the pretty jar of sweet, flesh-colored powder, the pots of rouge and rows of lipsticks. And then all the jewellery and silky things in the top drawer. I talked incessantly and upset her by wanting to put on her high heels and lipstick.

"Anyway, back to this first attraction. A cousin, twenty-something, from another city was staying with us while he looked for a job. On this particular day, I insisted on taking my nap on the living room sofa instead of in my bedroom. I remember sleeping for a while and then waking to see my cousin in a recliner chair across the room, reading a magazine. I thought he was very handsome, although I'm sure the word 'handsome' had not yet entered my vocabulary. So, what did I think, exactly, or feel? I think I simply sensed that 'otherness.' Well, I pretended to stay asleep, hoping he would look at me. I thought I was very beautiful with my eyes closed—that was my first notion of being beautiful, eyes closed—not looking, but being looked at. Why is that do you suppose? Anyway I kept my eyes closed, imagining that he was looking at me and admiring me the whole time, which, of course, he wasn't doing at all." She paused. "Excuse me, is that the bathroom?"

"Yes, go right ahead."

"And then I should go. You must be tired." She got up from her chair stiffly, holding her hips like an older woman, and disappeared into the bathroom. When she emerged, she began to pick up the empty tumblers.

"Wait. I have a question for you. Sit down a minute. But first, would you hand me the bottle, please?" Claire poured her tumbler half full. She was beginning to feel itchy again. The irritation seemed to come in waves. Dora had sat down again, this time more comfortably, cross-legged on the floor. "Do you think that's strictly a female reaction, that wanting to be looked at? Wanting to be an object almost?"

"Yes. I think the feminists are off base when it comes to that. Females want to be objects. I know this. It's the key to their sexuality. Men do not. Trust me. I'm an expert—on both."

"And you, as a photographer, make objects of everything. You know, there was a voyeur back in Kythera always at the same spot, above a cove where I liked to swim. I hated his spying on me, at least until I got used to it. Then I really didn't mind his being there. I even saw him as almost—um, a kind of protection. Now there's a question. Would a voyeur compromise his position by stepping in to help if his 'object' were in trouble?"

Dora laughed. "Would anyone?"

"Another question."

"Just ask Aunty Dora anything."

"At the taverna yesterday you said something about men and their mountains. That they were in love with their mountains, or something like that. What did you mean?"

"Well, last year when I was here, I had an affair—with a shepherd, in the White Mountains. I was taking photographs of the countryside and came upon his hut. I don't speak Greek, and he didn't have a word of English, but somehow we managed. And he didn't mind my—my ambiguity. They're a horny bunch, deliciously rustic. Did you know shepherds were a traditional cure for infertility?"

"How?"

"Apparently, in the past, when a woman couldn't conceive, she would wander in the hills. Then when she became pregnant, it was generally accepted that she'd been raped by one of the many pagan gods still roving the countryside. What else could explain it? Infertility was considered to be the woman's problem, never the husband's, so only a god could do the trick. The pregnancy was the result of a shepherd's rape, of course, and everyone sort of knew that, but, since it was the only route to a family, there was a collective denial about it."

"Does it still go on?" Claire thought of Eleni's childlessness.

"I don't think so, but who knows?" Dora was stacking the empty tumblers on the plate. "Gotta go."

"Thank you, Dora. Leave those. I'll walk down with you now." Dora preceded her down the stairs and opened the front door to the sultry evening. The fan in the bedroom had given Claire a false sense of cool motion in the air.

"Ta!" Dora was at the gate, turning back to wave goodbye. "I'll check in tomorrow."

Claire watched her walk quickly down the road. It was still light, and she looked up to the mountains, above which the clouds loomed darker than she had seen them since coming back to Greece. After doing some dishes, she went back upstairs, and fell asleep. Hours later she woke up, itching with the intensity of pain, and turned on the lamp. She had scratched her arms in her sleep, and there was blood on the sheet. It was three-thirty. Claire went into the bathroom, had another cool shower, and applied the cream the doctor had given her. Then she climbed back into bed. Still wide awake, she thought of Dora and her story of shepherds raping childless women. Like gods. Like Apollo. Apollo and Daphne—Eleni. Of course, that was how it had happened!

16

The swaying bus of celebrants passed under the huge arch that had been blasted through the rock by centuries of wet winds. And then, around another curve, a stretch of the sea opened before them, suddenly, and the blue expanse they were used to seeing in smaller pieces, in bays and coves, was as shocking as a friend's nakedness. Far below them appeared, in a walled and tree-protected place, the red roofs of the monastery that had been built for the Myrtidiotissa. A shepherd had found her icon in a myrtle, had picked it up and taken it away, only to lose it and find it again in the same bush. It was not there; then it was. He imagined it walking, and he imagined it flying, but, of course, it had done neither. Paintings had neither legs nor wings. What had occurred was beyond his thoughts. What had occurred was miracle. And so the church was built, a home for the black-faced madonna. It seemed that shepherds, in their closeness to the earth, were always stumbling upon such things. They had come upon the cave where the Christ child lay. They were the discoverers and messengers of the fabulous.

Eleni and her mother sat side by side on a jiggly torn seat at the back of the dusty bus, their basket of meat pies and a striped melon at their feet. It was hot. All the windows were open to catch the breeze of the moving vehicle, yet the women still held the bodices of their dresses away from their skin and fanned their ample cleavages with handkerchiefs. Eleni would not try to get into the church for the service, as she had the year before. It had been so hot and close with the press of the crowd behind her that she had thought she might faint. This year she would be happy to stand in the courtyard on the edge of the group and hear the service over the loudspeaker.

Every year Eleni made a special request of the madonna. The year before, it was to restore her grandfather's health, but the bus had just passed the graveyard outside Kalokerines where he was buried. He had died the previous winter, the day before her seventeenth birthday. On that morning she had not awakened as usual to the sound of his crossing the courtyard, but to a dog's bark that came later, and when she looked at her watch, she knew something was wrong. They had found him in his bed, on his side, hands folded under his head like a child, in the position in which he had always slept. But he had not been sleeping. And now he was mingling with the earth. Or with God. Which? Was that order or disorder? Perhaps it was wrong to ask the virgin to go against nature. Old people died; it was the way of things. Today she would ask for Kosta to love her. That, too, would be wrong but for a different reason. It was selfish. But her earlier selfish prayer for the disappearance of her rival, Pelagia, had been answered. The girl had moved with her family to Athens, and it was rumored she had found another love.

The road ended in a field. The passengers filed off the bus and took a crude footpath that led down through tall dry grass and thistles to the monastery. A few thistles were still green with fading purple flower heads, but most were brown, stick-like, and going to downy seed. Many of the islanders had already arrived and were milling about the stands that later would be selling food, drink and religious objects. Old model cars were parked wherever their owners had decided to stop, and donkeys stood tethered to trees, some still laden with panniers full of food. A number of pilgrims were camping, pitching tents in a grove of trees on the flat south side of the monastery and setting up folding tables and chairs. On the north side, through an arcade of plane trees, was the village, site of that night's festivities. Many celebrants had come from the mainland, and some had been staying for days within the monastic walls, in small cells consisting of nothing but a bed. They would have prayed, fasted on fava, horta and dry bread, and remembered to give thanks to the madonna for past miracles.

As the bells began clanging, people jostled their way through the courtyard towards the entrance of the church. Eleni moved aside to let everyone pass, something she often did, even when it wasn't important to be last, for wanting to be first was something she had never understood. She caught sight of Kosta up ahead, handsome in a bright red shirt, but he had not seen her. She felt a close warmth at her back and turned around to see Aleko. He had not given up bothering her, nor asking her to be his wife. His mother grabbed his arm and yanked him forward with the crowd. The courtyard was an ocean of sweaty flesh, and while earlier its air had been fresh, a potpourri of oleander and pine, it had begun to smell of armpits. Perhaps it would have been more pleasant inside the church after all, for there at least the rosemary-scented smoke of the incense overpowered any other smell. Thinking the virgin wouldn't mind, she left Tula and stepped just outside the gates of the arched entryway.

Eleni looked around the deserted area, the single vertical cypress among the other rounder trees, the leafy olives and fat pines. She had forgotten if one could see the sea from there, a fact that had not been important in past years. Now, for some reason, it was. Her changing perceptions of the world could be measured by the August celebration, to which she had come every year of her life, with the exception of one year, her tenth, when she was in bed with the chickenpox. Eleni could remember when the festival was to her nothing but a carnival of the senses, a place of new colors, shapes and sounds, plentiful food and affectionate grown-ups. Then when it was an exciting place for games such as hide-and-seek, and, later, a forbidden place to explore. She remembered the thrilling, self-induced fright when she and a friend thought they might possibly find their way into the dark subterranean reliquary, where the icon had been kept during the war. Then the religious fervour when she was eleven and twelve, followed the next year by doubts and a new awareness of life's contradictions. About that time, too, she began to think of boys and marriage. The feast day became an opportunity for romance. Some of her friends would meet their boyfriends after dark among the trees. Her friend, Ana, on this day the year before, had opened her legs for her boyfriend, Stefan, and then they had married. This was what happened, for the girl was then considered spoiled for anyone else.

Eleni moved up the hill a few yards to see if she could spot the sea and decided it could not be seen from there. She looked back to the tall, handsome cypress, the wooden cross over the entrance to the monastery, and the limestone bell tower jutting high above the roofs against the blue sky, its natural yellowy color a contrast to the immaculate white stucco of the monastery itself. The belltower was absolutely masculine, sexual. Was everything biology? Could we ever get beyond that? Was there anything beyond that? Eleni thought that the celebration brought forth a composite of all those feelings of past years, and she revelled in the new breadth and dimension of the experience. It was still a bright carnival, a place of gothic adventure and sexual romance, a time of hope, a meditation on the miraculous, but accompanied, in equal part, by doubts about the miraculous. The black face of the Myrtidiotissa had become, for her, a symbol of these contradictions. But even her doubts added spice, enhanced her sense of fullness, her intoxication with life and its possibilities. She was happier than she had ever been.

Hearing the first intonations of the priest come through the loudspeaker, Eleni returned to the entrance and looked over the heads in the jammed courtyard towards the source of the sound. The first response came rolling through the crowd like a wave. Many more such waves of sound and gesture followed, and, when it was over, the celebrants separated to make a path for the procession. The priest appeared first, looking solemn and bored, automatically waving the smoking brass censer as he walked. He was followed by the Panagia, escorted on each side by white uniformed men from the coastguard. Eleni had observed that the gold chasing on the icon appeared richer and more brilliant in the dimmer light of the church. In daylight it seemed ordinary, a part of nature, related in some way to the hot liquid sun. At that moment, she changed her personal symbolism. The black faces of the madonna and child would no longer represent her doubts. They were, after all, unlike the gold surrounding them, extraordinary. Like caves, they told of something beyond the imagination.

Behind the icon marched a motley and cacophonous brass band of adults and children wearing white hats with gold braid. The throng, carrying branches of fragrant myrtle, followed the principals around the monastery and then back into the yard where the priest censed the high pile of bread loaves on a cloth-covered table. After partaking of the holy bread, the crowd dispersed, moving in every direction for their midday meals, to the village, to the beach, to the grove of trees. Eleni, her mother and some of their relatives planned to have the afternoon meal down near the sea on a long, narrow strip of beach shaded at one end by the face of a cliff. Then there would be a collective siesta, taken in all sorts of casual postures, many drunken, and, later, more food, music and dancing into the night.

It happened later that evening. Eleni and Tula were sitting in the village square among relatives and neighbors enjoying the cooler air and watching the performances of various folk dance troupes. After the exhibition, everyone would dance—polkas, waltzes and modern forms like "the twist" to popular recordings from Italy and America. Perhaps Kosta would ask her to dance. He had paid her more attention since Pelagia's moving away, always coming up to their table at the Sempreviva and asking after her whenever he saw her mother in the Chora. Tula faithfully reported these meetings to her daughter, knowing her heart, but she also encouraged her to be kind to the annoying Aleko, who had tried to kiss her at last year's festival.

Eleni had just seen Aleko on the opposite side of the square with a gang of friends. Kosta was sitting by himself, only a few yards away from where she and her mother sat. Eleni put her hands to her hair. The braids were gone, her dark hair cut into a new and stylish bob. She was beginning to feel chilly and realized she had left her shawl on the bus. It wouldn't take long to go back and get it.

She found her way to the bus quickly, for beyond the lights of the village her path was lit by a bright half-moon. The bus smelled of hot plastic, dust, and wine, and she had to step over the bodies of two snoring men on the floor. She saw her shawl where she had left it, next to the basket with the remains of their picnic. Putting it over her shoulders, she walked back through the bus, taking care not to wake the men, and hurried down the path with anticipation. The shawl was new, her mother had embroidered it for her birthday, and she knew she looked nice in it, the white wool setting off her dark hair. Kosta might admire it.

She passed the monastery and entered the arcade of trees that marked the entrance to the village. The exhibition dancing was over. She could hear, over the loud chorus of the cicadas, strains of a popular piece. "Let's do the tweest, like we did last su---mmer—." Then there was someone behind her, hot breath on the back of her neck, an arm wrapped tightly around her stomach. A man's voice told her not to cry out. It would not have mattered *anyway, her practical side told her, for she could not be heard over the music and noise of the crowd. But then she realized the voice belonged to Aleko. She did not understand, but she was relieved. He was a familiar. She was not threatened. This must be some strange sort of game.*

He dragged her into a bushy area on the side of the road and fell instantly on top of her. Beneath them was a prickly bed of dry pine needles. "Be quiet," he implored. "I love you. I must do this." Then she knew. This is what had happened to her friend, Ana. But Ana had wanted it. Eleni tried with all her strength to get away, but he was too much for her. As she tried to repel him, he managed to raise her skirt and pull down her underpants. Her upwards thrusts to throw him off imitated the motions of sexual need and invitation. Nature seemed to conspire in this way. When she realized there was nothing she could do, she gave up the struggle and tried to block out what was happening, closing her eyes, making herself numb, making herself just another black beetle on the ground, or a bush, or tree. Eleni kept her eyes tightly shut and felt the rush of warm liquid between her thighs. She gasped, taking in a fishy smell with the pine-scented air, and then she felt him get up. Aleko zipped up his trousers and, without a word, walked back through the brush to the road. Eleni pulled up her underpants and pushed down her skirt. Then she lay there for a while, her heart still pounding in her chest. Her vagina and thighs hurt, but he had not entered her, at least not far. But he might as well have. Her future was immured in this single act. He would tell Maria, his mother, and Maria would tell Tula. She would have to marry him because now no one else would have her. It was the custom.

Eleni rose from the ground and looked around for her shawl. It lay against the pine, like a ghost of her past self, glowing in the moonlight. She picked it up. It was torn and covered with pine needles. Wrapping it around herself, she started back to the bus, unable to face anyone yet. Her mother would finally come looking for her, and she would say she had fallen asleep. This was true in an awful way. Tomorrow she would tell her what really had happened.

17

On Tuesday the wind had started up in the early morning hours. Claire awoke to the soft ruffling of the pages of her writing tablet beside the bed. Then there was a loud, dull clapping noise, like wood against stone, and the wind's intermittent wail over the steadier hum of the fan. She rose to unplug the fan and then returned to bed, letting nature's rhythmic, windy music lull her back to sleep. In the first daylight, she was outside the house, in nightgown and sweatpants, in an agitation of wheeling birds, bird-artists making evanescent shapes against the backdrop of shrub and sky. Claire, too, felt enlivened by the motion of the air, its caressing coolness and promise of wetness.

She yanked off the offending shutter that had become loose at one end and leaned it against the side of the house. Storm clouds were scudding at a fast rate through a pale sky in the north, and the southern mountain peaks were hidden from view by a solid gray scrim. The graceful fig tree, with its loopy trifoliate leaves, was swaying, and she picked some of its fruit, laying it on the ground to be gathered later. Claire trudged down to the stand of trees by the riverbed. How many rains, she wondered, would it take to fill the rocky flume. The storm, she knew, would bring George back to her. They could not explore active caves in the rain. The galleries could suddenly fill with water, allowing no room for escape.

Picking up the figs, she returned to the kitchen and drew a small serrated knife from a divided tray on the worktable. She cut the dusty purple fruits in two, marvelling at the red-brown flesh that would prove so deeply sweet, sliced some bread and put an egg on to boil. Then came another banging sound, this time from the front of the house. Another shutter, she thought, leaving the kitchen to inspect.

But the knocking was someone at the door. Eight-fifteen. Dora? George, already?

"Zoe!" Zoe and Harry were standing before her, smiling apologetically. She knew they might come that day but assumed at a later hour.

"Aren't you going to invite us in?" Harry asked, handing her a still-warm loaf of bread.

"Oh, sorry. Please, I didn't expect you so early." Claire stood aside, gesturing them into the room. They nodded emphatically to her offer of coffee. Zoe looked weary. She drew up one of the rush-seated chairs to the table and lit a cigarette.

Harry followed Claire into the kitchen where he inspected her bites. The disfiguring swelling had come down, but scabs were beginning where the bites had been.

"They found you delicious, didn't they?"

"The worst is over, thank God, and this cool air is a balm." She poured the hot water over the Nescafé and turned off her egg. "It's just about to rain, don't you think?" They carried the cups into the sitting room. "Where did you stay last night?" she asked, handing Zoe a cup.

"A guest house, in a village not far from here. We got lost last night trying to find Scala. You wouldn't believe these roads after dark. No light, no signs. It's impossible to know where you're going. We just gave up. And the guest house was awful. Lots of bugs, horrible beds, and another guest, a poor Albanian man, was sick and flushing the communal toilet all night long. Harry and I ran into each other roaming the halls at five this morning. We made plans to leave as quickly as possible at daybreak. We've just had some bread and jam at the taverna in Scala. The loaf, by the way, is from Manolis. He told us how to get here."

"He also brought us up-to-date on you," Harry said. "Your bites, the fact that George has gone—."

"And that Dora is here," Zoe added, smiling. She yawned. "I'm so tired. I didn't sleep at all last night."

"Why not go upstairs and get some sleep now?" At Claire's suggestion, Zoe put her coffee down at once and made her way up the stairs. "I just need to get dressed," Claire said, following her, "and then you can have peace and quiet as long as you want. By the way, can a woman be raped and remain a virgin? I've heard the hymen can still be intact after sex. True?"

"Yes." While Zoe stripped to her underpants, Claire straightened the sheets, which she had changed the day before, and found another pillowslip in a basket of fresh linen. She put on jeans, T-shirt and a cardigan and checked her daypack for comb and drachmas. Zoe was burrowed under the sheet and blanket, looking blissful. Claire closed the shutters and transferred a kiss from her hand to the back of Zoe's head before going downstairs. She wondered how soon George would be there as well. If he should arrive, Zoe and Harry could find rooms elsewhere. Harry was now coming through the kitchen from the outside with an armload of kindling.

"I thought I'd better collect some of this before it rains." He had found the scanty pile of wood against the back of the house. He pulled some yellowing newspaper from the basket by the hearth and placed the kindling in it. As Claire ate the breakfast she had almost forgotten about, he made several more trips for wood.

"Do you have a torch?" he asked. She found one in a kitchen drawer, and he flashed it up the chimney to see if the flue was open. Kneeling before the opening, he rumpled up the paper, made a tent of kindling, and lit a match. The wood caught just as the rain began to fall. Soon it was smashing against the roof, and the room grew darker. Claire went to the window. The rain was angled with the wind in the direction of the riverbed. She lit the brass candlestick on the table, the wrought-iron candelabra, and the oil lamp on the mantel. The room became a cavern of flickering light and dark, sweet with the scent of woodsmoke.

"There now. Cosy, isn't it?" Claire thought of George's teasing her about that word and felt a vague twinge of guilt. She couldn't deny the pleasure she felt being before a cosy fire in an unseasonable storm with her amiable new friend. While poor George——. "And what about you? Did you get any sleep last night?"

"Enough." They both sat on the floor in front of the meager flame, which was struggling to stay alive. "This rain. It's not usual at this time of year, is it?"

"No."

"I think Greece looks strange in the rain. So dark and wet. Not like Greece at all."

"Hmm. Not to me. Strange, that is. I lived here, you know, many years ago. Through two winters, in fact. But I remember thinking the same thing the first time it rained. Athens in the rain had seemed improbable. But there was something about it I liked very much—the strong mineral smell, I think. And the city lost its mythic quality. It became a real city with flesh and blood people trying to avoid puddles and stay dry."

Smoke had begun to flow into the room. The small flame sputtered and died. Harry got up and poked at the wood, failing to arouse a single spark. "I'm afraid the wood's too green. I'll try something from the bottom of the pile." He left the room, and Claire gazed into the dark hole of the fireplace. Where was George? When would he be with her again? She remembered Manolis saying he had the phone number. She had to find out. Harry returned with more wood. "This doesn't look much better," he said.

"Let's forget it then. I've been wondering about George. They usually don't work when it's raining. Why don't we walk into town? Maybe Manolis has heard something."

"All right. But why walk? I've got a car you know."

"I'm not afraid of the rain. Besides, there's a lull now. Let's get some exercise, and if the rain starts up again, we can get warm and dry in the taverna. Maybe have some lunch."

"Good. Let's go. There's a brolly in the boot of the car."

"A what in the what?"

"An 'umbrella' in the 'trunk' of the car," he said in a flat American accent.

"Oh, let me write Zoe a note in case she wakes up before we're back."

The rain had stopped, but the air was alive with wind and moisture. As they walked towards the gate, she noticed that the little garden was transformed, carpeted now with pink and yellow rose petals and bent by the force of the water, the daisies face down to the ground, the hollyhocks bowed and dripping. Harry lifted one loopy wet stem for Claire to pass under and they opened the gate to the road. While he went into the car for the umbrella, she checked the sky for weather signs. Towards the north, beyond the valley, there were tentative streaks of blue, but southwards the sky was gray and the mountain peaks, behind the town, still shrouded in cloud.

They started down the road. The landscape was vivid in the muted light, the road itself a rich brown against the glimmering gold of the fields and green of the trees. Beyond, in the gray mist of town, was a single splash of brightness, the electric blue of a plastic-tented fruit truck, a reminder that it was the day for fresh fruits and vegetables. As they neared the bridge, the rain began to fall again in large wet drops. Harry pressed the button above the umbrella handle, and it sprang open with a whipping sound to reveal a large gap where the fabric had come away from one of the ribs. He shrieked with laughter, and Claire understood. There was something amusing about the predictability of Greek things not working.

"Pure rubbish," he said, leaning the umbrella against the bridge parapet. "We can fetch it on the way back. Unless—perhaps we should go back and get the car."

"Not unless you want to. We're halfway there." She felt exhilarated by the walk and wanted to keep going.

By the time they took the turn into the village, the rain was coming down hard again. They could barely make out the objects along the way through the thick screen of the downpour. Claire was soaked. "Perhaps this wasn't such a good idea." She looked over to her companion, who seemed unperturbed. Happy, in fact—a child allowed to play in the rain. Anyway, Manolis would give them something with which to dry off.

154

He was standing on the step just outside his taverna talking to some villagers and, as Claire and Harry approached, expressed alarm at their condition. Of course they were wet, but Claire remembered the Greeks had superstitions about exposure to certain winds. Superstitions, or maybe they knew something she didn't. Manolis herded them up the steps, quickly opened the door, and pushed them before him into the room. Then he took the stairs to the upper floor two at a time and returned a few minutes later with an armful of towels and blankets. He had to leave right away, he said, as he placed the towels on the counter. A widow's roof had fallen in and he and some others were going to spread a tarpaulin. They could help themselves to whatever they wanted in the way of food and drink.

Claire grabbed his arm. "Will you please call George, or the project, before you leave? I'd like to know if he's coming back today." Manolis went behind the counter to the phone on the wall, picked up the receiver, and replaced it.

"Dead. It happens sometimes in this kind of weather. I'll try later when I get back." As he left, he nodded to a shadowy corner where someone was sitting at a table. It was Dora, smiling widely, obviously enjoying the scene.

"Don't you two know better than to be out in this? Come over and sit down." Harry crossed the room, and Claire ducked behind the counter to remove her wet jeans and T-shirt. She hung them on drawer knobs in front of the orange bars of an electric space heater, blotted her hair and skin with a towel, and wrapped a large blanket around herself.

On Dora's table were her camera, several rolls of film, and a pitcher of white wine. On one of the chairs hung a yellow rain jacket, hat and umbrella. Her rubber boots were side by side against the wall.

"You're prepared," Claire observed, taking it all in, feeling stupid in her blanket.

"Always, dearie. I never know how long I'm going to be anywhere, so I'm always ready for cold and rain. Especially since I have to be out in it."

"What have you been shooting?" Harry asked, with genuine interest.

"Oh, the village, villagers. There was a flock of them in here— men—when the storm began. You know, the gathering of testosterone to meet the challenge. I don't know Greek, but I picked up on the excitement about the storm, the wonder at the unseasonableness of it, and the problems it can create—leaky roofs, stopped-up gutters, small vineyards suddenly under water. I got some good shots I think."

"Black and white?" Harry asked.

"No, color. The light today is fabulous. You really need the sun for black and white. For the shadows. I came back here when the rain got heavy. Have some wine." Harry got up and went to the counter for tumblers. Claire watched him pick up a towel and pat his hair and neck before returning.

"Are you interested in any particular subjects?" Harry continued to question Dora, who was still busy organizing her rolls of film. He aimed the pitcher towards Claire's glass, but she covered it with her hand.

"No thanks." She turned to Dora for one of her cigarettes. She had put some in her daypack but had discovered that they, too, were wet. Claire was getting anxious about George. She had thought he might be back by this time, but now she remembered it would take a long time just to get out of the cave. She promised herself that she would not leave the taverna until she had communicated with the project.

"—icons," Claire heard Dora say. "I used to follow them, you know. You probably heard about the photographer who drove Jackie Onassis into obtaining a restraining order against him. Well, I was almost as bad. I was Jackie-crazed, too, and I ran into the other photographer everywhere. It became a kind of joke. We were competitive, but companionable too—both of us, so to speak, drinking from the same trough. I made piles of money selling those pictures, enough to relax for a while and begin the medical stuff. And then I just lost interest. Maybe it was the introduction of female hormones. I no longer relished the chase. I turned to this—interesting landscapes, townscapes and people. More reliable, more artful, and less dependent on chance. I have a contract now with an English publisher."

"Why 'icons'?" Claire asked, thinking of the religious ones. Dora looked puzzled. "I'm wondering why that word—you know—applied to people like Jackie or Marilyn Monroe?" She pointed to the old calendar on the wall.

"Because they're worshipped, I guess."

"Yes, but why are they worshipped? What traits do Jackie and Marilyn, for instance, have in common with religious figures?"

"They're one-dimensional, maybe?" Dora paused. "Or we perceive them that way. They're emblems. Marilyn was—is (they don't die)—a sex symbol. And nothing we know about her contradicts that. The idea of a fertility goddess doing ordinary things, driving, cooking, reading, is absurd. Maybe that's why she was so good in comedy. And Jackie—that's something else. The perfect lady, the epitome of civilized femininity— beautiful, dignified, religious, just intelligent enough, fashionable."

"Very good," Harry said. "And Diana, Princess of Wales?"

"That's easy," Dora replied. "Beautiful princess victim, right out of a fairy tale. You know how they were always threatened, locked up in towers and so forth. Well, she'd been locked out of the palace. And then her violent death positively sanctified her."

"Then an icon," Harry put in, "must be without idiosyncrasy. She, or he, must be the incarnation of an ideal without 'personality' or 'character.' Without complexity. There's a kind of vacancy, isn't there, that is perceived as positive?"

Claire agreed, thinking of the wide-apart eyes of the two American idols and the empty eye of Dora's camera that would swallow up a subject and spit out an object, black holes. She left the table to check the phone again and got a dial tone. She hadn't expected it so soon. And now Manolis was gone, and she had no idea how to reach the project. She hadn't asked for the number and would have to wait. The rain had stopped again, and Dora, waving a cheery goodbye, left the taverna to take some more pictures. Harry and Claire sat smoking, lost in their separate thoughts.

A sharp ring broke the silence. The phone and no one to pick it up. Claire ran to it and Harry followed. There was a lot of static and a rush of Greek words she couldn't understand. She asked the man if he could speak English, and he hung up. Claire and Harry were returning to the table when it rang again. This time Harry went for it. Claire stood in the middle of the room. Harry stayed on the line. He looked at her intensely, then turned his back to her, his left hand over his ear as he bent over the phone. She moved closer to him. Still no words from him, but nodding as if in comprehension of what was being said. He replaced the receiver quietly. He stood there for what seemed a long time, his back to her still, and bent slightly. She could read him. Her entire body began to shake. The room receded. Harry came to her and took her in his arms. She buried her face in his damp brown shirt. She knew.

"George."

"Yes. That was Colin Green, the project's hydrologist. There's been an accident," Harry said gently. He took her to the table and sat her down. He poured her a little wine and encouraged her to drink. "George fell down a shaft. They haven't gotten to him yet, but they're fairly certain he could not have survived. Stay here. I'll find Dora. She can give you some dry things to wear, and I'll fetch the car. Will you be all right for the moment?"

"George. Oh, no. No!" Claire shouted into space, accusing it, challenging it to contradict the awful fact. Perhaps there was a mistake. *It had to be a mistake.* In a few minutes Dora appeared, coaxed her from the chair, up the stairs, and through the hall to her room. Claire lay down on the bed while Dora pulled some clothing from the closet. Claire wanted to die, but she couldn't die, nor could she rest. She was filled with a demonic energy but, at the same time, felt unable to move. Dora helped her to dress, and she stood up. "Oh, it can't be!" she moaned and fell back down on the bed, unable to withstand the sheer weight of the knowledge.

"There now, Claire, come with me." Dora led her like a sleepwalker back down the stairs, and they waited together by the door of the taverna. Harry stopped the car, and he and Zoe got out. Both looked stricken. Zoe embraced Claire. She was crying.

"We'll go back now," she said. "I have some pills that will help you rest."

"No!" Claire was striking out at Zoe. "I have to go to George. Take me to him, Harry, oh, please!" Now she was sobbing and pulling at Harry's clothing. He looked helplessly at Zoe, who gently took Claire aside.

"We'll talk about it, arrange something," Zoe said soothingly, "as soon as we get back to the cottage. Colin is coming down right away, and he'll know what to do."

Colin arrived at the cottage around four. Claire had ignored Zoe's pleas to take a sedative. Colin was, for her, a final hope, and she wanted to be awake when he arrived. He would tell them that there had been a mistake. Caves were dark. It had been another man. Or a misunderstanding in the phone communications between those in the cave and those outside. Or, even more likely, Harry had misunderstood over the interference on the phone line. These things happened. She hadn't asked Harry for any of the details he might have been given during the brief phone conversation for fear he would say something that would plunge her into despair. They placed the straight chairs in a circle and, with Zoe and Harry on each side of Claire and holding a hand, listened to Colin.

"A piton that was supporting George's ladder came loose. The rock isn't always that solid, you see. It can happen. The area they'd been through was dry. They hadn't realized that the new region was as weakened by water as it was until—." Colin bent his head and was silent for a while. "George, who was the first to descend, fell through the shaft to the surface below. He was just about five minutes into the climb when he fell. We tried to reach him by walkie-talkie, and there was no answer. Two men scrambled down after him, the one who had the most first-aid training going first. It took them about half an hour

159

to get down, just to show you the length of the shaft. They never got there, for just as the first man was a few feet from the bottom of the shaft the water came rushing in, a flash flood, immediately filling the space to the roof, making it impossible to get down into the chamber. An end of rope ladder was floating on the top, and the man nearer the bottom made a grab for it, hoping it was connected to George and he could pull him up, at least keep his head out of the water. But it was just a loose segment. It wasn't connected."

"And then—?" Colin looked up at Claire's first utterance since he had arrived. "You don't have him—the body?"

"Not yet. We're hoping the water will soon run through to a lower level. If the space is a cul-de-sac, though, the water will stay there indefinitely. In that case, we'll have to get divers in from Chania to retrieve him. We suspect it's a fairly deep area."

"What's your guess?" Harry asked. "Enclosed or not."

"I hate to say. Most are not. In that case, we can probably get him out of there fairly soon." Colin folded his arms over his knees and stared at the floor.

"Why were they there at all?" Claire was challenging their safety measures. "George told me you don't explore active caves in the rain." Perhaps she could blame someone, even sue. And as she thought this, she knew there would be no solace in it.

"It wasn't predicted, you know, the rain, and they had only this to do before they planned to leave the cave and take a few days off. Besides, even if they'd known, a first rain doesn't usually bring about such dramatic changes. They'd have probably gone anyway. And it's even possible the rain isn't to blame. Something simply may have given way." Zoe had gone into the kitchen and returned with a steaming cup of tea. She handed it to Colin.

"And, now," she said, coming over to Claire and taking her hands, "you have to sleep."

"Wait." Claire waved her away. "Colin, how can you be sure he's dead?"

"Well, he fell several hundred feet. He must have died instantly. But if, by some chance, he didn't, he would have drowned in the onrush of water."

"Claire," Zoe pleaded, standing at the foot of the stairs.

"What if—." Claire paused to construct the scenario. "What if he didn't hurt himself that badly in the fall? What if somehow he'd managed to break the fall going down?"

Colin interrupted. "Remember, we tried to reach him on the walkie-talkie and couldn't."

"He dropped it in the fall—it broke. So he's down there and conscious and hears the water coming. What if there were a gallery or shaft above the area, more accessible than the one he'd descended, where he could get higher than the water?"

"Unlikely."

"But not impossible?"

"I'm sure impossible," Harry said, coaching Colin, not wanting her to entertain false hopes.

"Unlikely," Colin said again.

"Well, considering everything you've told me, I think there's a slim chance he's alive." Claire got up from her chair and crossed to the window. There was a loud crack, and a bright thread of lightning split the sky.

"We have a fresh crew camping above the shaft," Colin said, following her with his eyes. "They go down and check the situation every few hours."

"When are you going back?"

"Tomorrow. Harry and I will sleep at the taverna tonight. Zoe is staying here with you."

Claire walked over to Colin, still seated in his chair, and kneeled before him. "Colin, you must promise me something, before Zoe gets me upstairs and drugs me into oblivion."

"Yes."

"I want to go to the cave with you tomorrow."

"Do you know what it's like?"

"Yes, and I don't care. I have to be there." She stood up and looked helplessly around the room. "There is nothing of George here, you know. Nothing!"

Colin and Harry lowered their eyes. Zoe went to her and, arm in arm, they climbed the stairs.

18

ZOE MADE CLAIRE BREAKFAST AND carried it upstairs on a tray. It was ten o'clock. Claire had awakened in the middle of the night in spite of the doctor's ministrations, and Zoe had forced upon her yet another pill, promising she would rouse her when Colin arrived. But she hadn't. Colin had come by at seven-thirty with Harry, and Zoe and Harry decided that, rather than wake her from a drugged sleep, they would take her to the cave later on that day before returning to Chania. Harry then went back to the hotel to call Alex and Zeno.

"Are you sure you want to go up there?" Zoe asked as Claire picked at her scrambled eggs.

"Yes," Claire replied, putting the tray aside and rising from bed. Zoe followed her into the bathroom.

"There's nothing you can do for him now."

"I can be there for him if he's still alive." She mumbled the words through the toothbrush in her mouth and spat the foamy stuff into the sink. She wished she could vomit.

"Claire—he's not." There was a silence. Claire looked into the mirror and saw Zoe's face behind hers, speculative, assessing her state of mind.

"Well then, I can collect his belongings." Claire rapidly gathered her things that were in the bathroom and tossed them into the plastic cosmetic bag she had placed on the toilet seat. "And receive his— his body." She resolutely zipped up the bag and stared at Zoe in the doorway so that her friend would move aside. Zoe followed her back into the bedroom.

"Come back to Kythera with me. Colin will keep us posted. We'll make him promise to call us daily. Please." Claire reached under the bed for her large duffel bag and began stuffing her clothes into it.

"Look, Zoe." She turned around to face her. "I won't stay here after I know, after they—find his body. All right? What's today?—next Wednesday, if that has happened, I'll return to Chania. On Thursday I'll fly to Athens and then to Kythera. You can meet the afternoon plane." Claire felt marginally better making some plans. She had packed the bag so haphazardly that there was no room left for her books and papers, so she would carry them separately. She saw her last scribblings about Eleni. How remote she now seemed, how insignificant. Claire zipped up the duffel and looked around the room. "This cottage is a mess."

"It's not too bad. Anyway, Colin said not to worry. On our way back through, Harry and I will tidy up a bit and return the key to Manolis."

"Oh, I almost forgot." Claire tore a sheet from the yellow legal pad on the bed and wrote down her California address along with a hasty note, asking Zoe to give it to Dora. Zoe took it and put it aside. Claire then remembered the clothes Dora had loaned her that were still hanging in the closet. She pulled them out and put them under the note. Zoe looked regretfully around the room.

"Colin said he's going to sell this place. A pity, isn't it? It's so sweet."

Claire could no longer see it that way. Silently, she picked up the duffel and let it slide down the stairs after her. Zoe followed, with one hand on the bag to minimize the bumps. Claire checked the kitchen for anything she might have forgotten. The eggshell of the egg she had eaten the morning before—before the news—was still in the sink, a fragile artifact. Her eyes surfed the sitting room. She had collected everything, she thought. Harry was at the door. They locked up and walked down the front path. The hollyhocks were vertical again. The sun was shining on a rain-freshened world.

They were soon climbing the road to the cave. A mountain peak rising above a layer of cloud looked like a rough-hewn temple in the sky. They passed the shepherd's hut where she and George had been guests for breakfast, and she saw Panyiottis in the distance, his back to the road, gazing upwards. Was he looking for his sheep, or at the sky, or towards the mountain where he had discovered the cave? They were in different time zones, the shepherd and she. He lived in the past because he didn't know about George. They passed the point where George had parked that day, so they could hike to the view of his cave. George's beloved cave, his grave, his grave cave. Uncharted indeed. She remembered her first reaction to the little cave in Kythera. "It's like a church." "All caves aren't cosy," he had said. *Boum* echoed the Marabar caves, and Mrs. Moore had seen the abyss.

The car was slowing to a crawl. The sheep and goats had vanished. There was nothing for as far as the eye could see but cracked rock. The karstic phenomenon. The notion that rock was solid, impervious, permanent was an illusion. It was soluble, friable. All it took was water. They were approaching the summit, and she knew they must be close to the cave. After a bend in the road, there was a sign on the left and, below that, on the downslope, the roof and top half of an angular modern building.

"Well, here we are," Harry said, looking around, grimacing slightly. He parked the car alongside a jeep on the asphalt area between the road and the building. They got out, and Harry took her duffel bag from the floor of the back seat. They descended a flight of painted brown steps to a single utilitarian door that looked to be the only entry.

It opened into a large room with a high ceiling. The opposite wall was almost entirely dirty window, through which shone a formless white sun. A noisy wasp was beating itself against the glass, trying to get out. The ground outside the building sloped downwards and levelled off to a point where they could see treetops, indicating perhaps a more fertile swale in the rock beyond. Just below them was another building running perpendicular to theirs. The ski lodge was bleak, a ruin of cheap materials, and it reeked of stale smoke. A white vinyl sofa, flanked by matching chairs, faced the fireplace in the soot-stained wall on the right. In front of the sofa was a rectangular coffee table with several metal advertisement ashtrays, spilling over with cigarette butts and ashes. At the other end of the room was a table for dining, with folding chairs scattered around it, and beyond that the kitchen. An open staircase led to a second-floor exposed hallway with doors at regular intervals. The bedrooms, Claire realized, the windows of which had to be facing the parking lot and road.

"It's awful," Zoe said, looking around and then again at Claire. She looked as if she were going to try to talk her out of staying, but thought better of it and walked to the window. "It's more like a military compound than a recreation area." A door opened above, and an unshaven heavyset man in an undershirt and shorts came to the railing and looked down. He yawned, scratched his chest, and said something to them in German.

"Do you speak English?" Harry asked him in German. "We are friends of George Vrilakis."

There was a pause while he absorbed the information. "Oh, please wait." He re-entered his room and appeared a few minutes later fully clothed. They heard a car above in the parking lot. The German came down the stairs, and Claire approached him, explaining that she was going to stay and asking where she could put her things. He looked sceptical. She didn't know if it was because he had not understood the English, or because he had. Just then Colin came in from outside. Her heart jumped, for she knew he had come from the cave. She studied his expression, and it told her there was no news. Colin led them silently up the stairs to her room, George's room, and Harry deposited her bag. She wanted to cry. It looked like a prison cell. There was a single bed with a thin worn mattress, on top of which was a pillow and a flannel-lined sleeping bag. On the bag was a coarse gray blanket, unfolded, hunched up as if something alive were underneath. George had slept there, on his last night above ground.

"Are you sure—?" Zoe asked.

"I'll be fine." Claire wanted them to go then. She wanted to be alone with George's belongings. "I'll see you in a week—promise." Suddenly, Claire realized she wouldn't be seeing Harry, who was returning to London. "And, Harry, God knows when I'll see you." She felt the sting of tears and let them come. Everything she had known was dissolving. That she would see Zoe in Kythera in a week was incomprehensible. That she would ever see Harry again, impossible. Harry, too, had tears in his eyes. Dear detached Harry, blinking the water away furiously. He wrapped his arms around her and kissed the top of her head. Zoe embraced her, and Claire stood at the door watching them descend the stairs. They gathered by the outside door and spoke quietly for a few minutes. Zoe and Colin were doing the talking. They seemed intimate, at ease for strangers. Zoe and Harry left. Claire closed the door to inspect the room.

On the chest of drawers, in a thick layer of dust, was an alarm clock, a woollen knitted cap turned inside out, and an out-of-date Italian magazine with a mountain climber on the cover. She picked up the cap, closed her eyes, and buried her face in it. It smelled of him, his hair and skin.

She opened the drawers of the chest. The top one had a tablet, pens, pencils and a detailed map of the cave. The second, a jumble of underwear, sweatshirts, batteries and a wallet. The wallet contained a few thousand drachmas and a scrap of paper with the word "Scala" and a phone number. The taverna number, of course. More tears. Her eyes felt fat with them. The bottom three drawers were empty, and she transferred some of her clothes from the duffel into them. Then she opened the closet. Coveralls she hadn't seen before, still in the shape of George, familiar cotton shirts, and, on the floor, a spare red helmet with a headlamp and his unzipped, empty duffel bag. She hung up her jacket, a sweater, and a second pair of jeans. As she picked up George's bag to move it aside for hers, something, with a bright flash, fell to the floor. In the dim light, it looked like some sort of tool, and she bent to pick it up. It was a sheathed hypodermic needle. In the bag was an open cube-shaped package full of cylinders that looked like pen cartridges and more needles. She pulled out one of the cartridges and put it back. The writing on the package was in English: "Insulin."

Claire was dizzy with this sudden knowledge, the onslaught of answers to questions that had not really surfaced, but had been, nonetheless, always there. She lay down on the bed, acutely aware of the fresh soap smell of the pillowcase, for which she felt a tweak of gratitude. She was trying to piece things together. George had been an insulin-dependent diabetic. Why hadn't he told her? And how could he possibly have explored caves? She knew a little about the disease and its dangers: weakness, blurred vision, possible seizures, coma. Diabetics could lead fairly normal lives, but exploring caves was a risky occupation. Having the disease had been George's secret, not only from her, but from his fellow cavers. Otherwise, he could not have done this thing he loved to do. He would not have been hired.

She thought then of some of his peculiarities—his abrupt and brief disappearances, his abstention from sweets, his unquenchable thirst. She saw George and Zoe in the hallway of the hotel in Chania. Yes, of course: Zoe had known. Perhaps she had helped keep him supplied with insulin, tested for sugar in his blood. Claire sat up, animated by the discovery. She had now solved the puzzle of George's walking fully clothed out of the sea on her first day in Kythera and his phony story about being trapped in high tide. He had run out of insulin, of course, or had forgotten it in town, and had made his way back the quicker way. It was a twenty-five minute walk, but only a five-minute swim. She remembered Zoe's comment about his carelessness. It all made sense now. But why did he choose to be a spelunker? It was almost suicidal. She remembered his comment about feeling closer to God when exploring caves. Did his disease have anything to do with the accident? With a pang of disillusionment, Claire silently accused George of irresponsibility.

"Things are often known for what they can do without." She remembered his words about the hearty little sempreviva flower. There were things George could *not* do without. He was horribly dependent. Claire lay back down and cried long and hard, after which she felt sedated. Then came the sound of a car in the parking lot, and she climbed on the bed in order to see out of the high window. Several men with canvas bags were spilling out of a van. A rubber flipper protruded from one of the bags. The divers had arrived. They would deliver to her what she had come for. She raced downstairs and out to the parking lot.

Colin and Claire sat in the front seat of the jeep with two of the Austrian divers in the back. The road that wound upwards to the cave was rutted and steep. They had been driving for only a few minutes when they came to a makeshift barrier in the middle of the road, a two-by-four stretched across two sawhorses. There was an official sign with the no-trespassing symbol and, scrawled in white paint on a large boulder on the side of the road, the word "private." Colin pulled on the brake and jumped out. He removed the barrier and drove the jeep forwards. He then jumped out again and replaced it. Within minutes they were in front of the cave. The oblong hollow in the rock was on the bias, an ugly slash leaning to the left, as menacing as the maw of an angry wild animal. This was not the legendary cave where Zeus was born and fed by bees. It was real, a blunt fact of nature. And yet Claire felt that if she stood there staring at it long enough, it might yield its secret. It would tell her about George.

The Austrians were putting on their helmets and attaching carbide lanterns to rings in their coveralls. They were speaking in English, double-checking each other, making sure they had all the items necessary for their expedition. Their voices were low but their words distinct, magnified by the drumlike effect of the surrounding limestone. Colin was talking into a telephone receiver just inside the entrance of the cave. He hung up, walked over to the jeep, and pulled out a package of chocolate cookies. He looked at Claire apologetically and said "biscuits" under his breath. He handed the package to one of the divers, who stuffed it in his rucksack. The divers then disappeared into the cave.

Claire stood there with Colin, looking at the hole, at nothing. It did not give her the answers she had come for. It was intractable, not an opening but a dead-end. It was an implacability she had mistaken for permanence. She found it exasperating to stand there before the cave and not come any closer to the truth about George. What hope or mad superstition had led her to believe that proximity might bring knowledge? She would, of course, have to wait. Colin told her they might have some news in the morning and now she must return to the lodge with him.

The days were getting shorter. It was evening and not quite dark. The sky was a deep blue-gray, almost purple. Claire wasn't hungry but knew she should eat, so she entered the large kitchen and began to forage in the cupboards. She found what she took to be a can of soup from behind some boxes of cereal and rice. There was no longer a label on the can, but the size and liquid movement within it suggested that it was soup. She pulled out drawers in search of a can opener and found one whose round cutter was encrusted with blackened tomato sauce. Claire held it under the hot water faucet and, when it was clean again, opened the can to find a clear broth. A saucepan sat, ready to go, on one of the six burners on the greasy stove. She began turning knobs and, failing to bring forth flame, lit a match and placed the pan on the fire.

When she returned to her room, she climbed into the sleeping bag to keep warm. Later, she heard voices from below and the clatter of utensils against pots or plates. The residents were either cooking or having dinner. Who did the cooking? If there was a system here, it had eluded her. The men were alien to her. She felt more isolated from them by reason of gender than language or purpose for being there, although those factors also divided them. In a place like that, she felt more sharply the division between male and female. Perhaps rapport between the sexes could flourish only in a comfortable, secure world. She was not sure why that was, if it was. She wished Zoe were still with her. Or even Dora, who would be above with her, not below.

Claire had put some books beside the bed. She picked up one for company, for consolation perhaps. Maybe for sleep. It was the Forster book. "A miracle of creation!" she had enthused to Harry as they sat in the garden in Chania. She couldn't bring herself to read anything now, all those words, sentences and paragraphs strung together in the attempt to create "something." She closed the book and thought of Larkin's "total emptiness." Hardly a consolation, but the nihilism brought a sort of numbing sensation, an emotional deadening that worked on her like an anesthetic. She sank into the welcome emptiness of sleep.

She woke up in the last darkness before dawn and watched the shapes in the room slowly emerge, a re-enactment of creation. She pondered again the idea that had come to her as she listened to the music of the lyre-player, that it might be the only point to life. Shape, form, an end in itself, always before us, but shunned as we search futilely for something more. And she had dreamt again of the Madonna of the Myrtle. Her image haunted her. Her faceless face was an imageless image, a formless form. Why had it stayed with her?

There was a white glow over the chair, her T-shirt. She would wait for everything to announce itself before going down the cold hallway to the fetid bathroom. Then the face of George's alarm clock appeared. White was visible first.

Someone rapped on her door. Colin softly called her name. She sat up, suddenly alert, and wrapped the scratchy blanket shawl-like around her before telling him to enter. He opened the door and stood silently in the frame. He didn't have to say anything. In the dim light she couldn't read his expression, but she knew the news was bad. They had not found George, he said, but they were certain of one thing—he could not be alive. He warned her, in a taut voice, that it was important to understand that, to have no doubts or lingering hopes. He explained in a matter-of-fact tone that the divers had had to abandon the search because the floor of the gallery was dangerously uneven. Furthermore, rain was forecast. The project must close down until the following spring.

Claire could see his face more clearly then. He seemed uncertain whether or not to cross the threshold. He was embarrassed, distressed to be the bearer of such news, wanting to give comfort but not to assume intimacy. She reached out to him. Courtesy required it. Colin entered the room, took her hand in his, and said he was leaving in an hour for Scala. She could go with him, catch the bus, be in Chania by late afternoon. She agreed to the plan, and Colin made to leave. At the door, he turned to her and suggested that she might wish to take something of George's as a keepsake, adding that there was another pot-holer on the project from Malta who would, on his return home, call upon George's relatives. Colin then closed the door quietly, apologetically.

She trekked down the hall to the bathroom and, back in the bedroom, packed her things. Everything was ready to go. Claire wanted nothing of George's but, remembering the needle and insulin in the closet, knew she must dispose of them. Keeping his condition a secret from the other cavers was one last thing she could do for him. She took the plastic bag holding canvas shoes from her duffel and replaced them with the needles and insulin refills, intending to put them in the kitchen trash on the way out. As she looked around the room for anything she might have forgotten, she saw a piece of paper—the yellow, blue-lined type on which she normally wrote— lying on the floor at the foot of the bed. Claire thought it had fallen from her bag and picked it up. It was the bottom half of a torn sheet, and there was a single line of writing at the top, George's handwriting: small, modest, precise. *The invisible must be understood by the visible.* A runic message, a sacred puzzle. This she would keep.

THE SEMPREVIVA

Aftermath
February 2002

THE GREEK WORD FOR WINTER IS "keemonas" with the accent on the "moan." It sounds like keening—it sounds like the wind. The storms this year have been unusually strong, tearing off roofs and shutters, uprooting trees. Orchards and vineyards have been ravaged, and the open seas are treacherous. Even the bays are swollen and rough, the beach at Kapsali entirely under water. All the seaside places are closed, their doors and windows boarded up, and fishermen spend their days playing cards and dominoes at the inland tavernas. Waves rush up and over the low seawall in front of Eleni's café, where I sat months ago, basking in the sunshine and the imagined certainties of the life here.

Zoe and I are sharing a basement apartment in the Chora. It's a natural cave beneath a shop that sells replicas of icons, costume-dolls and plates with helmeted warriors to tourists in the summertime. The rounded walls, whitewashed and hung with handwoven fabrics, divide the space into three rooms, the bedroom where Zoe sleeps, the sitting room where I sleep, and the kitchen where we spend most of our time together—a cheerful place with bright oilcloth on the table, bunches of dried herbs dangling along the window above the sink, and raffia wine bottles dripping with candle wax on every surface. Flokati rugs, still smelling of goat, lie on the floors, and kerosene heaters keep it warm.

The inhabitants of the Chora recognize me now, the American woman who stayed beyond the season—even after her country had been attacked. But they know nothing of my private sorrow, that my presence here is, in fact, a kind of ritual, a vow I've made to remain until spring. "To deprive tragedy of its impact," I explained to Zoe. "How grand," she replied with a dry smile.

I am still working on my story of Eleni. I rarely see her now because

I've stopped the Greek lessons, having come to prefer the embracing sound of the language to the understanding of it (one does seem to preclude the other), and I have not ventured down to Kapsali. When I see her from time to time here in town, I am startled, as if my heroine had suddenly materialized before me, for although the Eleni of my novel is no longer Eleni Pappadopoulos of Kythera, her physiognomy is precisely that of the real one. We always stop to exchange pleasantries, and I sense a change in her.

Zoe and I have over these autumn and winter months settled into a routine. Every weekday morning she crosses the square to the clinic, and I pull up a chair to the small desk in the sitting room to write. I often look up from my work just to listen to the wind. Even in our subterranean rooms I can hear it howling as it drives the rain through the narrow street above. Unless I have errands, I stay here until Zoe's return for lunch and after that, weather permitting, set out for a walk while the town sleeps. Today I hiked to the old fortress, mainly for its encompassing view of this southern end of the island. Far below, the harbor looked deserted, motionless except for the relentless waves and a single flock of seagulls circling above the lighthouse, their distant cries piercing the silence.

I can imagine Kapsali in spring. Once again the waves will subside and fishermen tie up to the sea-blackened jetty. Sailboats will put in for shelter and, later, the brazen whistle-blast of the Costa line will announce the first of its weekly visits. By then all the cafés and shops will have opened their doors and inhabitants and visitors alike crowd the waterfront. Once again Eleni will set up her pavilion by the seawall, and Alex and Zeno will arrive every evening to watch the sun go down. Once more—but by then I'll be gone.

I remember those evenings well, the long, late light, the fortress darkening to silhouette as the sun sinks behind it, the smouldering red sky and purple sea, the smells of boat fuel and squid frying in olive oil. I have not learned to let go. I can still hear the lilt of Harry's laughter though that is past. And the caver, vanished—George, who first appeared to me like a god, stepping fully clothed out of the sea.

When I left the fortress ruins, dark clouds had begun to gather in the north, and rain is forecast for tonight. The view of Kapsali had reawakened in me a keen nostalgia for the events of last summer, and, as I retraced my steps down to the Chora, I felt a strong craving for a cigarette. I had quit smoking on my return from Crete, believing I was pregnant. Zoe had given me the test and assured me it was negative, but I thought I might as well continue my abstention from tobacco.

I had been convinced that I was pregnant. It seemed eerily appropriate when I recalled George's telling me about the mating cicadas that reproduced and died shortly thereafter, and his explanation, on the day we picnicked at the cave, of the flamboyant first and final bloom of the doomed aloe. It is nature's way, telescoped. But he has died childless.

I checked my watch. Zoe would be getting up soon to return to work. I would write for a while and then prepare our dinner. She cooks on the weekends if we don't go to the Ladases' for the evening meal or eat at the souvlaki place next door. The restaurant has a television set which, other than the sporadic delivery of newspapers from Athens, has been our only contact with the world. We learn that the hunt for Osama Bin Laden goes on in the icy peaks of the Tora Bora. He is already the stuff of legend, the last sighting having been "a tall man riding a horse into the forest." They may still find him, or they may not. Does it really matter?

The attack on America occurred just a few days after I returned to Kythera, and my personal mourning became entangled with the larger event. The television footage of planes slicing into the World Trade Center and the towers dissolving into roiling clouds of smoke and flame, raining debris and mortal ash, was played over and over again. I thought of Yeats's "desolation of reality" and of George's uncanny reference to those twin towers, along with other things, as "not God" while we sat eating peaches at the harbor in Chania. Was he suggesting that the absence of them, in some strange way, is?

After the cave accident, Colin Green escorted me back to Kythera and then stayed on a few days before returning to London. He is a compassionate man, and although I appreciated his support at that terrible time, I was not so blinded by grief that I failed to detect the pretext. Nor had George's death, as affecting as it was to Colin and Zoe, dampened the growing ardor between them. On the contrary, I think the seriousness of the circumstances under which Zoe and Colin met, their mutual grief and the reminder of the fragility of life, served, rather, to nourish the seedling of their desire. It was clear from the moment Zoe met us at the airport that something had passed between them. Colin has flown down from England twice already, once in October and again for a few days at Christmas. George, I know, would have approved. So much for Larkin's "total emptiness" of death.

Harry Smythe has sent me postcards from time to time, typical Harry-like messages, snippets of poetry, philosophic musings, his usual extravagant compliments mixed with affectionate inquiries about my health, my state of mind. Sometimes I wonder if he, too, has ulterior motives. Certainly I am fond of him and grateful for the attention.

There have been times over these winter months when I have felt somewhat reconciled to George's death, when I see his demise not as an ending so much as a demonstration of something he had been trying to show me all along. It is a strange thought, but it is almost as if he had died before he actually died—if he has died. George sometimes assumes for me an almost fictitious quality, as if he had been a kind of metaplot, someone who had had no real existence other than to augment or explain ours, but I can take it no further than that.

I turned into the little cube of a post office and bought a postcard to send to Annabel. I had already sent her every card I thought might appeal to her: the goat, the ubiquitous cats, the donkey, the pretty flower-filled window-boxes, the sunny beach. For variety I was forced to buy "Kapsali at night," all black hills, rose-colored roadways, and white buildings lining the womb-shaped bay, with bright yellow lights becoming green as they fade into their reflections in the blue-black water. I asked the postmaster if there was any mail for Zoe or me. He handed me a letter for Zoe from her mother and a postcard for me. I placed them both in the pocket of my cardigan. I would wait until I was home to read the postcard.

I opened our door and descended the flight of steps to the sitting room, leaving Zoe's letter on a small table at the bottom. Always anxious to hear from Colin, she looks there first when she comes in. I placed my postcard from Harry on the daybed, removed my sweater, and went into the kitchen. I pulled out the lamb chops from the refrigerator to come to room temperature and checked the cupboard for pasta. Then I poured myself a glass of wine and returned to the sitting room. The image on the postcard was a portrait that hangs in the National Gallery of the late Iris Murdoch, a writer Harry and I both admire. The card was slightly creased and had a small coffee stain on it. I was amused. I knew this had not happened en route but before it had left Harry's hands. I turned the card around and was disappointed to find only a brief quotation and the sign-off. I had come to look forward to Harry's words. The words were not those of the writer pictured on the other side, but from a poem by Yeats. *Out of a cavern comes a voice, /And all it knows is that one word 'Rejoice!'*

"I saw Tula Karvouni this afternoon," Zoe announces. "Flu. It's all over the island." We are sitting at the kitchen table after dinner, gnawing on salty lamb chop bones in the flickering candlelight. A strong wind has come up, and our electricity is out. At the sink when the gale began, I stood and watched for a while the sticks, leaves and bits of litter skipping along the eye-level street, some of them flying, and the occasional pair of feet running for cover. Tula Karvouni is a change of subject, for Zoe has talked about Colin all through dinner, her hopes for a future with him, her fears of losing him, her speculations about why he hasn't written. It has been a week since his last letter.

"How is she? Otherwise, I mean."

"Very, very happy," Zoe says, licking her fingers. She grasps the decanter of red wine and, with an exaggerated sweep of her arm, pours us both some more. "I'll begin at the beginning. Do you remember the day we left here for Crete? It was August fifteenth, remember? The holiday?"

"Yes."

"And how Tula hurried off after dropping Eleni at the airport? She was going to the festivities at Myrtidion, to the panegyrie. Well, like all the other celebrants, she prayed to the 'Myrtidiotissa.' And, like every year for the past God knows how many, she prayed for a grandchild. And—." Zoe relishes revealing her news in tantalizing bits.

"And—?" I lean into the table.

"Her prayers have been answered."

"What? You mean Eleni's pregnant?"

"No."

"Well, what?"

"Eleni's not pregnant. But she is going to have a baby."

"What?"

"Do you remember that day at the airport, that she was going to Athens to meet her cousin, Serena, who was coming over from Australia?"

"Yes."

"Well, Serena, it seems, has had a difficult time. She's single, has two children by her former husband, and when she met Eleni in Athens was pregnant again and unclear about the identity of the father. To make matters worse, she's unemployed, and her widowed mother is seriously ill. The only reason she came to Greece was to plead with Eleni to take her child and raise it as her own."

"And she's agreed?"

"Yes. The baby was born in November—a boy. Serena is bringing him over in April." Zoe rises from the table and takes two of the guttering candles to augment the light at the sink, crying out as she spills a bit of hot wax on her hand.

Beyond being very happy for the Eleni of Kapsali, I am trying to imagine her as a mother and wondering, at the same time, if such a thing could happen to the Eleni of my story. Would the Eleni of my story happily raise a child with a man who had once raped her and with whom she has since had no sexual relations? I take the plates to the sink and scrape the bones into the plastic-lined garbage bin.

"Oh, and there's something else." Zoe immerses the dishes in soapy water. "The Pappadopouloses have inherited an old taverna. It's on the road between Kalamos and Livadi. Hasn't been used for years. Apparently, it's on land owned by some branch of the Karvouni family, whose only surviving member died this winter. Actually, it belongs to Tula, but it will be passed on to Eleni and Aleko, and they're fixing it up right now. They're opening in the spring. If they can't get enough help, they may have to sell the café in Kapsali."

"Was the taverna called the 'Sempreviva'?"

"Yes, a big yellow building with the letters still on it. Oh, something else—. I found this today, lining a shelf at the clinic." Zoe wipes her hands with a towel, enters her room and reappears, waving an aged sheet of newspaper. "It's about the fire, the freighter fire that brought George here. I know you'll find this interesting."

The news item had been extracted from an Athenian English-language publication. There is a good color photograph of the flames rising from the boat, sending into the brilliant pink sky a dark plume of smoke. That evening Alex and Zeno were at Eleni's, as usual, watching the sun go down and have described for me the scene—the fishing boats drawing together at the mouth of the bay, the urgent voice on the port's loudspeaker warning them to disperse, villagers gathered along the seawall, gesticulating and speaking in loud, excited tones, barely audible over the pounding of the helicopters, moving in and out of the black cloud and buzzing overhead on their way to the airfield. All this I have imagined many times. Yet the article still holds a piece of information I was, until now, unaware of— the actual date of the fire. My decision to come to this island and George's rescue occurred on the same day last year. I know this because it is Sophie's birthday, and I had attended an afternoon party for her, during which I recall announcing my intentions, a decision I had come to just a few hours before.

May 2002

THE ATHENIAN WOMAN WHO OWNS the shop above our rooms has arrived and, with a loud clattering of keys and strenuous pushing inwards of the warped door, reopens for the season. I race up the stairs and follow her and a one-eyed cat into the cold, damp shop. She throws open the shuttered windows, letting in daylight from the street. Casting her eyes about, she takes inventory and runs her finger over the top of the glass display case. Then she passes through an arch into a small office where she fills a *briki* with water and places it on a hot plate. I eagerly purchase a small replica of the "Myrtidiotissa" and a flashy silver necklace to wear this evening. I am the *Kyria*'s first "tourist." George would be amused. I also buy a book that will help me identify the wildflowers of Kythera.

It is finally that time of year. The long rainy season has brought forth a heady profusion of flowers. The yellow broom, of course, tall, lush, and sweet along the roadsides and occasional brilliant streaks of red poppies. Vigorous vines of blue convolvulus snake their way through crumbling masonry, and the greeny-white spread of Queen Anne's lace looks, from a distance, like foam on a sea of grasses. We are already into May, and still there is the occasional rain, large, sloppy drops of water bringing out the smell of wild fennel and polishing the island until it gleams.

I ask the woman where I might find fine linens in Athens. Zoe is marrying Colin in June, in the Glyfada church where she was christened. It is going to be a large wedding, attended by relatives and friends of Colin's from England, as well as two or three generations of Stefanides and their friends. Byron and Mina have returned from France and are giving the couple a reception in their rose garden. The day after the wedding, I am leaving for California.

I pick up my purchases from the counter and, thanking the *Kyria*, step out of the inky shadow of the shop into the bright morning. It rained again in the early hours, and the white walls of the Chora shine clean in the honey-colored light. Four old men sit together on a bench against a sunny wall across from the square. The aroma of baking bread fills the air, and I take the few steps up to the street above ours to the bakery. There is a great flurry above the door as a pair of swallows dart back and forth to the beginnings of their nest in a drainpipe. The baker's wife is just now retrieving the loaves with a long-handled wooden spatula. I buy a crusty round loaf smudged with charcoal, which Zoe and I will have for lunch. The Sempreviva reopens tonight, and we are having dinner there with the Ladases. Colin, too, if he makes it. It is a big occasion for Eleni and her family, in fact for everyone on this side of the island, particularly those who remember it from before.

The day is so lovely that I am torn between sitting idly for a while in the square or getting back to my writing. I look over to the empty benches under the pine trees and then to the road leading down through town. Even the narrow strip of macadam is sparkling in the sunlight. I decide in favor of work, for the evening promises to hold enough pleasures. Maybe even Harry, who has announced he is coming to Kythera some time in the next few days. Harry's plans are always a little vague. I am hoping that he has been in touch with Colin and will arrive on the same flight.

Back in our rooms, I take the bread to the kitchen and then slide my fingernail under the sticky tape to release the icon from its envelope of blue-patterned paper. I stare at it for a long time and then look around the kitchen for a place to put it. Not finding one, I take it and the other packages into the sitting room. Sitting on the daybed, I stare again at the black face, this strange image that is, at once, something and nothing.

I remove the silver necklace from its tissue wrap and put it on. It is the first personal item I have bought in over a year. Remembering the full-length mirror in Zoe's bedroom, I enter there and stand in front of my image. A stranger looks back, a not-unattractive one. I allow myself this, for it has been a long time since I've given much thought to my appearance. Height is a good thing as one gets older, and I am thin. There is no superfluous flesh obscuring the essential roundnesses of my womanhood. Function still defines form. The shine of the necklace echoes the shine of my still-dark, thick hair.

It is strange the way I have moved in and out of this body. The time, during my pregnancy, when my mind was buried in it, co-opted by it, and I felt the lassitude and serenity of an animal, darkness and sleep my allies. And, later, when consciousness became unmoored, floating away from the body into a strange and fearful country, naked without the animal protection of it. I was depressed, sleepless, afraid of the dark. The two extremes. And now I feel in balance, healthy again, unafraid yet feeling the normal tensions of life. And, for the first time in ages, I am appraising myself as a younger woman might, trying to see myself through someone else's eyes, a photographer's, a voyeur's, a lover's perhaps.

The knoll on which the Sem>previva sits is as barren as ever. Even the interminable rains have failed to bring forth much in the way of vegetation, but there is a good deal of life within the storm-battered structure. Music floats through the open door as well as the shrill crying of a child. As we walk up the dirt path to the entrance, I notice that the walls are still a pocked and fading ochre, but the large block letters have been repainted in a bold poppy red. Eleni comes over to meet us, eyes smiling, arms full of colicky infant. Aleko is behind her. He, too, smiles. Driving over this evening, Zoe hinted to me that sometimes the baby comes before the sex, adding, with a wry smile, that professional ethics prevented her from saying more. Tula rises from a table, where she has been talking with a local farmer, to collect her grandchild, and during the transfer I touch the soft, round cheek, distracting him for a moment from his discomfort.

The walls have a fresh coat of white paint, and there are floral curtains at the windows. The lacquered pine tables and chairs are new, and a bar with high stools has been added in one corner of the room, a concession, I think, to tourists who will travel up the road from Kapsali in search of an inland, "more authentic," taverna. The Ladases are sitting at a table against the far wall, watching the silent images of a soccer match on television. They see us and wave us over. Zeno pours wine from a bottle of Boutari red, and Eleni brings us cheese and olives. Other customers arrive in parties, some bringing gifts to Eleni and Aleko. The surface of the bar is filling up with potted plants and cut-glass vases of spring flowers. Some men have come over to our table, which is the closest to the television, and stand watching, sharing comments with Zeno about the game. Zoe and I keep looking towards the door, hoping to see Colin and Harry walk in. Eleni has brought us a plate of boiled zucchini and a platter of roast lamb and potatoes. Her baby has stopped crying and is being passed joyfully from table to table. Greece has just scored a goal, and the men are cheering.

Colin walks in, and Zoe runs over to him. The absence of another person at his side brings a watery sting to my eyes. It is a purely physical response, of which I am conscious only after it happens. The severity of my disappointment surprises me. I bring my hand up to the necklace and caress the smooth, skin-warmed metal.

The lovers have an intense conversation by the door before coming over to the table. Colin leans over to say he must speak with me. We walk over to the bar, away from our friends. Colin has not come from England but from Crete. They are getting ready to go back into the cave for more exploration. The expedition to collect George, though, has already gone in. The water had drained to a lower level. He wants me to know that George's body has been recovered and cremated, according to the stipulations of a will he had left in Malta. It is over. I know the information is supposed to be comforting, what they call "closure." Grief counselors say we have to go through certain

185

stages. What Colin doesn't realize is that I don't require this. I had come to terms with George's death, and the finding and disposition of his remains are no longer important to me as they were in those beginning days of mourning. I had somehow already *placed* him.

Colin and I rejoin the others. I think about his news, its uselessness, its extraneousness to my present resignation. Colin tells us that George had refused to wear the life-line that cavers normally wear, which might, in this instance, have saved him. We are quiet for a while. The voices of the other diners and, again, the baby's cry intrude on our silence. Eleni gathers her baby from the lap of a customer and, holding him close, speaking to him in low, soothing tones, takes him towards the kitchen. There is paraphernalia back there, I know, a cot, a change of diapers. And now we begin to talk again, this time of a wedding.

I have awakened again. This second time I can't get back to sleep. It is still dark, and I switch on the table lamp beside the daybed. I pick up the miniature icon that is leaning against the lamp base and look at it, gazing for some time into its dark face. I am no reverent islander, hoping, by prayer or propitiation, to enhance my life. I am not asking for anything. I simply want to know. I think of the time I stared at the black mouth of the cave, willing answers, getting none. Perhaps if one stares long enough—. *I am not empty, I am open.* A line of poetry from God-knows-where. I replace the icon and turn out the light. They say if you need to sleep and can't, think of black velvet, of a sack of potatoes, of sheep. I think of crumbling towers, the icon's black face and its penumbra of gold. I sleep.

There is a gentle rapping at the door. I open my eyes, and see the soft gray of first light in the narrow high window above. Who is here? Zoe and Colin are here, I think. We came back together. They are in the next room. I shake my head to wake up, to get my bearings. I swing myself out of bed, put on a robe, and then stumble up the steps to the front door. I open it, and there is Harry with bags under his eyes, beaming, and smelling of cigarettes.

"It's a 'hat' wind," Harry says, running to retrieve my visor cap before it bounces over the edge of the empty pool. We have taken the road out to the unfinished hotel. "That's how the Greeks describe it." He hands me the hat and sits down beside me on a low ledge above the pool. "'Hat' wind, 'chair' wind, 'table' wind, depending on the intensity."

"The hawks are loving it." I have been watching them soar and bank on the solid windstreams. The sky today is alive with flying things: birds, small clouds, bits of last summer's litter, even a jet flying west, leaving in its wake a white trail in the blue. On the distant horizon are two wind-filled white sails. "There's a 'cucumber' wind too. But that has to do with moisture. And Zeno tells me the Greeks have ten different words for rock."

This is the first opportunity we have had to talk. Yesterday, minutes after I had let the exhausted Harry into our rooms, Zoe emerged from her bedroom, followed by Colin. Harry had come in on the early morning ferry, waited in Kapsali until seven, and then walked up the hill to the car-rental place on the square. Finding it closed and not knowing what else to do, he came to us. Zoe thought the owner was in Athens, but I was certain I had seen him the day before. Finally, Harry found him at his house, rented a motorbike, and left for the Ladases' to get some sleep. And now after the confusion of his arrival and the noisy ride out here on the bike, there is an awkward silence, the kind that stems from having too much to say. It is immense, charged with the baffling events of the last ten months.

"So they never found his body," Harry says.

"Oh, but they did. Colin told me. He's been cremated." Harry reddens. He looks dismayed. I can read him, and I think I understand. We've been told different stories. "You mean he just told *me* that?" Harry looks away. He stands up and pulls a cigarette from his pocket.

187

Turning into himself, away from the wind, he lights up. "What?"

"That was terribly clumsy of him," Harry says. "He obviously wanted to spare you, but he should have let the rest of us in on it!"

"Never mind." I put my hand on his arm. "It's all right really. I prefer the truth."

Harry, shaking off my hand, walks down to the pool's edge and stands there, looking down into the crater. He is angry at himself. After a few minutes, I join him. "Tell me everything you know."

"There's nothing actually, and that's the problem. They think he might have survived the fall and, perhaps barely conscious, crawled deeper into the cave, a place that was open then but is now closed. The only other possiblity is someone found the body before Colin's group got there." I think of Panyiottis, the shepherd, and instantly dismiss the possibility. "And both theories are implausible. They're utterly mystified by it."

I take a moment to assess my feelings about this. I am not upset by Harry's information. On the contrary, I prefer it to Colin's lie, but not because this is fact and the other was fiction. It is because, in this case, the absence of George's corpse somehow has more coherence than the lie of discovery and cremation. Colin's fabrication to console me held nothing of the magic that was George. This does. As my eyes begin to focus again, I see a tiny spot of yellow against the brindled stone on the far wall of the pool.

"Oh, look." I point to the flower. Harry looks at me and then at the flower. He understands now that he hasn't upset me, and he is smiling with relief. "It's a sempreviva. It can live without water, you know. Some things are known for what they can do without."

"Hmm. And some for what they can't do without. Let's walk down there." Harry points to the area around the cottages.

We make our way around the pool and down the slope leading to the edge of the headland. I have never been over this ground, the summer habitat of the voyeur, and I wonder if he'll be here again this year among the rocks, peeping out of the cottages. We find an area protected from the wind and a soft blanket of new grass on which to sit. "When are you returning to San Francisco?" Harry asks.

"Right after the wedding—the very next day, in fact."

"I've never been there." His voice is taut. I know Harry likes to go where he hasn't been. He would like an invitation. He plucks a stalk of grass and sucks on the end of it, and I examine a sprig of chamomile. I bring the tiny yellow-green bud to my nose, inhaling its wholesome, citrusy sweetness.

"You wouldn't like it, I'm afraid. Terribly crowded. And no real seasons. Everything happens at once. It's not uncommon to see yellow leaves falling from the trees and landing on roses still in bloom and budding camellias—three seasons at once. The flowers appear never sure when to do what."

"Quite." He swallows the word with a grimace. I think I may have hurt his feelings. There is a racket of flapping wings above us. One raptor is now chasing another. More noise. Swallows nesting in one of the cottages. "I know how they feel. The flowers." I have hurt his feelings.

"I would like to see you in San Francisco, Harry. Please come out and visit me. Of course we must see one another again sometime, either in England or California. I didn't want to discourage you, but to—prepare you."

"Look, I must say something, and it might as well be now." There is still tension in his voice.

"Of course." I brace myself. I am staring at the sea, letting the glittering corrugations made by the wind on the water absorb my thoughts. I know, on some level, what's coming.

"Do you remember that evening on the Ladases' terrace back in Crete? I told Zeno that I had dreamt I'd seen a statue, and he said I had met my ideal? The truth dawned then. I knew I had."

"Yes, I do remember. And you toasted Zoe with a line from Yeats." I laugh and give him a gentle poke on the arm. "'Live lips upon a plummet-measured face.'"

"You were already taken, remember?" Harry looks at me, challenging, beginning to smile. "Besides," Harry grins, becoming easy again, finding his old refuge in lightness, "Zoe Stefanides does have a beautiful face." He looks out across the water. We are quiet for a while. "I knew you recognized the poet," Harry resumes, "but the toast was a private tribute. To be understood, really, by no one but me. Because—I was beginning to understand, for the first time, my feelings for you." He says this matter-of-factly, tactfully, in a way that does not require the reply I am unable to give. But I am pleased by his declaration, and I want to choose my words carefully. I am beginning to see the possibility of another story.

"On the other hand, maybe you would like San Francisco."

Harry beams in response.

With a surge of energy, we rise and walk back towards the hotel. Yes, I think, climbing on the bike behind him, putting my hands to his waist. Yes, perhaps he will.